The Last Chord Concert

Stephen Shepherd

First Edition: 2020
Rs. 200/-

Cyberwit.net
HIG 45 Kaushambi Kunj, Kalindipuram
Allahabad - 211011 (U.P.) India
http://www.cyberwit.net
Tel: +(91) 9415091004 +(91) (532) 2552257
E-mail: info@cyberwit.net

Printed at Repro India Limited.

Contents

CHAPTER ONE

When Michael Molecule, the rock star from Neptune, found out that his manager Click Dark wanted to see him, he couldn't believe what his secretary was saying. His secretary, Emma Stark, from South Bend, Indiana, a brown-haired, eye-glassed, efficient lady, who had worked five years for Molecule Enterprises, was just relaying the message she had taken earlier that morning. Her office, separate from Mr. Molecule's, was located just to the left of his, and not far from the boardroom that adjoined both offices in suite-like fashion. It wasn't often that Emma entered Mr. Molecule's office. Michael Molecule was the foremost composer and guitar wizard in the galaxy, and he liked his privacy. And despite all the work, Molecule, she thought, had still maintained his youthful air. Now, he was thirty-one. A star since fourteen, many other people with his talent would have succumbed to the lifestyle that fame in the intergalactic fast lane brought. But not Mr. Molecule; his hair was still as blond as the day he had arrived on the rock scene with his first interplanetary hit "Shoot the Moon," a kind of narrative set to music about his now defunct love affair with Princess Phaedra of Saturn. The lyrics were undeniably brilliant, and the melody unforgettable, at least that's what all the critics in the solar system said, even Click Dark, the aging rock promoter from Pluto. But Click Dark and the others, even with their acclaim of Michael Molecule's first hit, didn't have the vaguest notion of how good the talented kid from Neptune really was; that is not until as many as two million fans jammed into the rock stadium near Tranquality Bay on earth's only moon to croon to his lyrics and stomp their feet at his rhythms. It was then that Click Dark, now grey-haired, realized what Molecule represented to the intergalactic music scene; that he was bigger than any single musician, group, or chorus of angels to come down the interstellar pike in many millenniums.

So, it wasn't by accident that Click Dark used his influence to become the manager of one of the hottest properties since moon rocks.

"Are you sure you took the telephone call right?" Michael Molecule asked, taking a seat behind his desk, stretching his long legs out in front of him.

"Absolutely, sir," Emma replied. "Click Dark distinctly said that he'd be leaving for Cygnus immediately and that you were to meet him at the Lyra Lounge at 11:00 a.m."

"But we won't have time to even consider the concert deal with Big Start Enterprises. It could mean millions. He didn't say any more?"

"No, sir, just that you were to meet him, and to be on time."

With that, Emma lowered the clipboard she was holding to her side and took off her bifocals. Her hair was pulled back, done up in a bun, and it was her sense of loyalty that prompted her to let the clipboard drop onto Michael's desk and walk around to one side of it. Her tan skirt was tight around her thin body as she walked, and her white blouse sparkled in the morning sunlight coming in through Michael's office window.

"Michael," she said after stopping. "I'm sure that Mr. Dark is well aware of the importance of the Big Star Enterprise deal and wouldn't call you away at this critical time unless it was very important."

"I know," Michael said, his blue eyes closing in thought for a moment, "but it's so unlike Click to throw everything up in the air like this, especially with such an important deal pending. We both know this could be the last big deal we'll both need to satisfy our dreams of rock and roll immortality."

As she stood there next to her boss, Emma knew that Michael's assessment of the importance of the Big Star deal was accurate. After all, neither he, nor his manager, was getting any younger, and lately she had secretly noted that it had been increasingly difficult for Michael to concentrate. That while his music was still very good, it wasn't as good as his early pieces, those written on the road in the back of an old intergalactic space bus. She sensed that Michael, after two years of seclusion, yearned once again for a live audience, and Big Star Enterprises had been working on nothing less than an interstellar gig that would once and for all launch Michael Molecule's name into every corner of the galaxy and rock and roll immortality. Behind his desk, he could not write the kind of music he wanted. And while all this was left unsaid between them, Emma knew what he was thinking, and a knowing glance ran between them.

"Okay, get Teaspoon Typhoon to fire up the space pod. I'll go over and see Click, but I'm not accustomed to being up-rooted like this in the middle of such a big galaxy deal."

On the way from his office down to the space pad, Molecule thought about his last statement. Emma, his secretary, following close behind, was thinking about it too. What irony, they both thought, as they marched towards the launch dock, that Michael should start to feel so comfortable behind his desk, while his music suffered.

* * * * * * * * * *

Big Star Enterprises was a rock and roll consortium that dealt with the speculative future of rock and roll music in the universe by the issuing of space bonds, a common stock that entitled the holder to a piece of the success, if there was one, or a piece of the failure. However, almost no one thought about the possibility of failure at the mention of Michael Molecule's name. It was true; he was coming out of semi-retirement and getting back on the road. And those who did doubt that after two years Michael had lost his touch were quickly convinced of both his talent and drawing power after a cameo appearance on Aid for Jupiter: A Hunger Gathering, at which he announced his return to one last chord in concert.

After the announcement by Michael at the Aid for Jupiter concert, the financial backing fell together so fast that investors had to be turned away from his office door. In fact, the phone had just yesterday stopped ringing, and Molecule once again had gotten a chance to concentrate on his return to one last live performance. Earlier this morning, before the subsequent telephone call, and the entry of Miss Emma and her message, Michael had been standing behind his guitar again, plugged into a wall of amplifiers, looking out his plate glass windows into the Cleveland sun. The blue sky was everywhere, hope in Michael's mind that his return to live rock would be a success. One thousand investors had lined up to back him, each sporting 2,000,000,000 Zercons that he would be. He couldn't let them down.

The doors of Michael's space pod opened, and he and Emma stepped in, the doors slowly closing behind them. Inside, the surroundings were instantly familiar. Both Michael and Emma, along with Michael's band "The Rocket Launchers," had spent many days seeing the galaxy from the luxury of its plush interior. To the left as they entered was the cockpit, from where Teaspoon Typhoon, Michael's long-time friend, and army buddy, piloted the craft. Michael, unlike other rock stars, had not fought the military draft when the war broke out on Saturn's third moon. And while he could have easily gotten an army job in the entertainment field, Michael, a man of honor, chose the infantry, and eventually became a laser gun specialist, training at Fort Icon on Andromeda. He eventually distinguished himself in the Battle of the Windless, where he had met Teaspoon Typhoon, his pilot, under the worst of circumstances. Michael was pinned down in a Zenith crossfire of laser guided light, number two yellow, and was the last man left in his squad of twelve, when Teaspoon, separated from his own unit, happened along, just as the Zeniths were about to overrun Michael and his position. Luckily, Teaspoon was a nuclear laser expert, and his hand carried a Quasar 12, which made mince meat of the Zenith onslaught, with most of them retreating as fast as they could. Michael, who couldn't believe his good fortune, ran to embrace Teaspoon, whose space pod was not far way, and they had been friends ever since. Yet, it wasn't until a few years later, right after Teaspoon had piloted Michael's last tour, that Michael found out that Teaspoon was a robotan, and not a human. But after they had been through so much, Michael still befriended the loyal servant, treated him like a brother, to everyone's surprise. He eventually bought Teaspoon's mechanical contract from the Prince of Brahe. Theirs, Michael had told many people, was a legitimate friendship, though an odd one by most people's standards. After all, humans had their place in the social strata of the universe, and robotans had theirs. But you couldn't prove that sociological fact by looking at the way Michael and his robotan buddy Teaspoon acted. If it weren't for Teaspoon's confession, however, most people wouldn't have even suspected him a robotan, something that had fooled Michael.

Most robotans used in and around the galaxy were built in Markab, near the Window in Pegasus from a rare metal accidentally found at the bottom of the Pegasus River, close to the Falls. A Pegasus fisherman, trolling for Spica in the river, struck Neutrolite, a synthetic substance deposited at the fall's base by industrial river deposits. Formerly sludge, over the years it had solidified into an indestructible metal stronger than any factory manufactured metallic. "It's nature's way of holding the upper hand," Michael had written in one song lyric, "a way that tells us go back to the land." And back to the land the metal speculators went, mining every portion of the Pegasus River. Within days, miners from all over the solar system arrived and threw up crude industrial complexes of sheet metal and fiber to extract the metal from the river's bed. "Never mind the crudeness of the building that surround the mine; the blackness of smoke that bellows forth," Michael Molecule wrote in "Blacksmith" a number one tune in the galaxy for twelve weeks, "just extract the ore; the gold in one soars." The song went on to describe the reaction of those early miners who arrived to stake claims and their difficulties in keeping them. No major veins were struck, however, although many fortunes were made, especially by those companies that manufactured robotans. When no major veins of Neutrolite were discovered, the companies wisely went to a scaled-down robotan, the four-foot model with the plastic head and green body. Almost no one today ever sees a robotan as large and that looks like Teaspoon, but then he was one of the first made, hence his human-like appearance and endless opportunities. Right after his six-foot tall construction of steel, Neutrolite, and glass, the Polaris Company of Pegasus, anxious to show off the endless possibilities of using robotans for the labor previously done by the slaves from Utrone, a lower form of humanoid captured centuries ago in the Wars of the Windless on Neptune, programmed Teaspoon's computer to a sophistication that makes most people's head spin even today. His I.Q. was 1,000; his physique stronger than sunlight, his wit and knowledge comparable to Kittsland, the Uranus playwright, and his loyalty unquestionable, something that Michael had learned, not only after Teaspoon had saved his life, but many times after while he was piloting his space pod through some of the worst space terrain imaginable.

In those slack years of Michael's career, the ones right after his release from the military, Teaspoon had to pilot an old Electrode 180. To this day, Michael and Teaspoon still laugh about the numerous times the damn thing almost killed them. But Michael's career had temporarily soured during his absence in the army, and his manager, Click Dark, had advised him not to live in the luxurious lifestyle he had lived before his military induction. "If you do," states an earlier Michael Molecule song, "you'll end up in ruin." So, while somewhat recognized as a rock personality, Michael was not totally known. So, Michael took his manager's advice and replaced his once lavish lifestyle with one of modesty by comparison and placed his faith in Teaspoon to fly him to some of the remotest corners of the galaxy in hopes of regaining some of his lost popularity. But now times were different, and as Michael entered his expensive, top of the line, space pod, Cosmos IV, and jerked back the curtain that separated the cockpit from the rest of the plane to nod at Teaspoon, he knew that he was almost there again, at the top of the rock and roll galaxy. But he wondered, as he took a seat across the isle from Emma, why Click Dark would jeopardize his meeting with Big Star Enterprises.

* * * * * * * * * *

Click Dark had been at the top of the universe's rock and roll heap since rock and roll's inception in the early 1950's. He had been one of its original supporters, even in its early going when rock and roll had been so crude that it would make your ear drums pop and was confined to the early ears of only human beings. Rock and Click Dark had come a long way in 3,600 years, and now Click thought, as he left his room at the Nebula Inn on Cygnus, and headed for the Lyra Lounge, where he would wait for Michael, he wanted to see rock and roll to its ultimate conclusion, a one chord concert struck in interstellar space by Michael Molecule as promoted by Big Star Enterprises. It would make both him and Michael rich beyond their wildest dreams, and he was as anxious as anyone, including Michael, to get a contract signed and get the show on the road. And until early this morning, things for the one chord concert had been exactly on schedule: The Comet Stadium, Vega at Zenith, Tuesday, August 4th, complete with an audience that read like a who's who of intergalactic rock stars with Michael playing to no less than 40 trillion people and 15 billion robotans. But then Click had received the phone call from Harry Sloan, his press man, and things had gone haywire.

Click was used to such setbacks, being no new face to rock promotion. After all, he was the one who put together the Live Galaxy Aid Concert, and had booked Michael into Pegasus' Great Square Lounge, opening for the McBison Brothers, an O-Zone Chute duo from the Northern Cross, right after Michael's release from the army. But this time, Click thought, sitting down in a chair at the Lyra Lounge to await Michael's arrival; this time, he had to handle things differently.

* * * * * * * * * *

Harry Sloan, a short, round-faced man, was Click Dark's up-front man, the one who did the paperwork, worked out the details that allowed the contracts to proceed. And Sloan had been the one who, for Click, had brought the negotiations with Big Star to their present state. For years Click had had the utmost faith in Sloan's ability, and that's why, he, too, was as surprised as Sloan at the recent turn of events that threatened to cancel their contract signing with Big Star.

"It's the weirdest thing," Sloan had told Click over the phone earlier that morning, "the contract was on the table; both sides were in agreement, and then this thing about Michael's friendship with a robotan come up. "To tell you the truth," continued Sloan, from the telephone in his motel room across the street from the Big Star headquarters, "I couldn't believe it, and for a moment I thought they were kidding. Then an attorney for Big Star, all decked out in a three-pieced suit, takes out an envelope, and spreads some photographs of Michael and his friend, Teaspoon Typhoon, the robotan, on the table, and says that they're getting some heat from Pluto about the racial mixing of Michael's friendship. I just about flipped and grabbed the contract, but was stopped by the same lawyer, who by now, I'd realized, was dead serious. Then he said,

"You wouldn't want anything to happen to our contract negotiations, would you?"

I said, "No."

"Good," he said, "Why don't you just tell your boss Click Dark to tell Molecule to get himself another flyer."

"And another friend," I added.

"Exactly," he replied.

"And if I don't?"

"Then, I think you can safely assume that Big Star Enterprises will not promote the deal."

"Great Cetus," I said. "Move into the 25th Century. Robotans, especially those as bright as Teaspoon Typhoon, have more brains and feelings than most humans I know."

"But that doesn't negate the fact that he is indeed a robotan, and not a human, and that makes it my responsibility to listen to Big Star's stockholders, who are telling me to get Michael to divest himself of his friendship with Teaspoon the robotan, no matter how bright, or they will withdraw their financial support."

"They would do that?" I asked.

"Absolutely," he said. "So, I came back to my room, and got on the phone to you, Click, as soon as possible to ask for instructions. What should I do?"

Dark thought for a moment, hovered over his telephone, covered it with his big hand. Then he said, "Tell them we'll get him to agree. I'll take care of it."

After his 8:00 a.m. conversation with his front man, Harry Sloan, Click Dark hung up the phone and then suddenly picked it up again to ring Michael, who he knew would be at his office awaiting the delivery of the Big Star contract. That's when he decided not to discuss the issue with Michael over the phone, but rather invite him, no matter how bad the timing, to Cygnus and the Lyra Lounge, where Click Dark now waited.

* * * * * * * * *

Michael Molecule's space pod had all the evidences of rock and roll fame and fortune. Its interior was covered with plush red carpet and Three Leaps Speakers, and a refrigerator cooling the best Equator Cocktails this side of the Summer Triangle. But neither Michael nor Emma, his secretary, availed themselves of any. They were both too worried about what Click had to say. They had both deduced by now that there had been some last-minute snag in the negotiations, some glitch that needed to be ironed out, and only could be after Michael and Click had conferred.

Cruising through the galaxy in interstellar space at warp speeds was Teaspoon's, the robotan's, specialty. He had originally been programmed for Cosmic Ray map reading, so his additional flawless programming and performance as a pilot was something to be envied. As his space pod lifted off, left earth behind, Michael knew how lucky he was to have Teaspoon as a friend. Looking out the window at the endless blackness of space, he knew he was lost from the word "go" and depended entirely on Teaspoon to get him where he needed to go. It, Michael thought, had been that way for years. He had come to depend on Teaspoon. There was nothing that Teaspoon wouldn't do for his human friend. In the wake of the rising and falling fate of a rock star's fortunes, Michael had really come to appreciate Teaspoon. Teaspoon's just being around made Michael feel more secure about his destiny, and that his was indeed the playing of the last chord that would put an end to rock and roll.

"Are you really sure you want to do it?" Teaspoon had asked him, not long after the negotiations with Big Star Enterprises had started.

"Do what?" Michael had replied from his office sofa.

"End Rock and roll by playing its last chord. It seems like such an unlikely thing to do, coming from someone who's made his living from one gig to another. What about the other musicians who are just getting started? Those that still have something to say, but for some reason can't get a recording contract, or booked into places like Mercury's Strata Lounge. What's going to happen to them?"

"I've thought about that," replied Michael. "Playing the last rock and roll chord in the universe does carry some weight. But timing, I've concluded, is everything. If the timing is right, then it was meant to be. If not, well then, you might as well not do it."

"And you think the timing is right for you to end it all?"

"If Big Star says so. Then I guess it is."

"What do you mean, if Big Star says so. There was a time when you wouldn't let the intergalactic corporate structure call the shots."

"Those days are gone," Michael replied. "Now, it's big bucks, galactic videos, laser albums, space pods, and promotion. Talent can get lost in all that mess. That's why I had to play the game as well. Who would have ever heard of Michael Molecule if it hadn't been for Click Dark. Let's face it, he controlled who made it, and who didn't from early on. Those who didn't see things his way, simply weren't heard from again. It doesn't take a dumb guy like me to get smart really quick, especially if he's got something to say."

Teaspoon, the robotan, ran his hand across his thick red hair, and wanted to argue more. But in the course of his events in connection with Michael's destiny, he had learned long ago that he did not chart the course. Robotans, after all, had no rights in intergalactic space, and he would have to simply agree with Michael's decision because it wasn't his, or any other robotan's place to dispute it. But Michael had long listened to Teaspoon's opinions, and he respected them in matters not so close to his heart. Click Dark and the promo machine had gotten him this far, and if they took him to playing the last guitar chord leading to the ultimate demise of rock and roll, it was his destiny to pursue it.

On an Orion hillside 220 light years away from Michael Molecule's space pod speeding towards Cygnus, Michael's meeting place with Click Dark, a team of space pod roadies had arrived close to dawn to set up the stage and the gigantic Three Leaps Speaker system that would carry Michael Molecule's last rock and roll chord into the electro-magnetic spaces of the universe. It was no small undertaking. Of course, the latest in red light proton sound equipment, light year spectrum tracking devices, and ultra-violet calculating equipment were being used, set up by the most knowledgeable sound team of robotans in the universe. Their take for their participation in the striking of Michael's last chord would easily bring each of the 10,000 workers luxury for the rest of their lives. But it was more than future luxury that worried Pinkus, the roadie crew manager. If Michael Molecule struck the last chord, then he and millions of rock and roll lovers would never hear another three-chord run. For Pinkus' design for intergalactic sound interaction included, under the instruction of Big Star, the intense focusing and conversion of sound into Far Infrared light that would not only carry the chord into the dark recesses of the universe, but would also destroy all knowledge of rock and roll from the eardrums of its listeners. The Far Infrared light waves would energize photons that would carry gamma rays to the furthest neutron star and melt guitars and pics. Hopefully, it might even convert former rock and roll addicts into lovers of the O-Zone Chute and the McBison Brothers, Big Star Enterprises' next group slated for intergalactic stardom. The McBison Brothers, Phil and Don, played mystical melodies on classical Chutes. Nice music. But to the die-hard rock and roll fan, it wouldn't sound like much. Filtered air through acoustic straw pipe only peeps. Yet, beyond the end of rock and roll, Pinkus, the chief roadie, worried about the fate of millions of robotans. Rock and roll had provided them with work, had taken them out of the ghettos of The Trapezium, and had promised them, for generations, a way to defy the odds and an economic system dominated by humans. But Pinkus, like the others on his crew, knew his place, and while he—and other robotans—had thought about preventing the concert, he was afraid to make waves.

* * * * * * * * * *

Michael Molecule's space pod, Cosmos IV, gently eased down onto the pad outside of Cygnus's Lyra Lounge, where Click Dark had waited patiently for nearly three hours. It was now 11:00 a.m., and as Michael and Emma deboarded into the time chamber to sensitize their bodies to Cygnus' atmosphere; Teaspoon Typhoon, the robotan pilot, checked the instruments, clicking switches. Teaspoon nodded when Michael pushed back the cockpit's curtain, then Michael told him that he and Emma wouldn't be long.

The walktube led from the time chamber directly into the Nebula Inn where the Lyra Lounge was located. Michael and Emma could have taken any number of existing tubeways, some leading into downtown

Cygnus, but they kept to their mission, and went directly to the Lyra Lounge where they met Click, who was hovered over his third Space Blaster, a mixture of three gas atoms from Nebula NGC 661. Click kept his finger over the top of the lid of his glass, saw his guests coming, then picked up the glass and tilted the lid in his direction, snorting.

"It must be real bad news," said Michael, "for you to be having a go at a Space Blaster?"

"Bad," grunted Click, setting down the glass. "I'll tell you how bad it is; this is my third one."

"Whe-e-w," said Michael taking a seat, and motioning for Emma to take a seat, as well as notes, of his conversation with Click. "So, what's up?"

"The worst," Click replied. "The Big Star Enterprise consortium is ready to back out of the deal."

"Why? I thought your man Sloan had everything under control."

"He did until this morning when the consortium through one of their attorneys added a new contract condition."

"What new condition?" Michael asked, looking directly into Click Dark's brown eyes.

"Click avoided Michael's stare, took another snort of his Space Blaster, then set the glass down. "On the condition that you'll cease your friendship with Teaspoon Typhoon, your robotan, and get yourself a new pilot."

"Wait just a minute," Michael said, his voice raising, and his blue eyes narrowing. "My friendship with Teaspoon has nothing to do with our deal with Big Star."

"But it does," Click replied. "Don't you see, the moment you became an intergalactic rock star your actions and attitudes were transmitted throughout the galaxy. And even today in many parts of the universe, robotans are not fully accepted as equals. Unfortunately, where they are not is where the majority of the stockholders from Big Star are from. It's simple mathematics: they don't like your attitude on this robotan issue; and they have the power to change it, or force the Last Rock Chord Concert, and all that it means, down the tubes."

Michael sat up straight in his chair, looked at Click and then at Emma, who had been taking copious notes the whole while. Suddenly, he said, "What do you think, Emma?"

Emma, taken by surprise, dropped her pen and scrambled to retrieve it from the floor. "What do I think?" she finally said, her head suddenly appearing above the table. "What do I know?" she said. "I'm just your secretary."

"Come on, Emma," said Michael, "you're much more than that. While I haven't confided in you as often as I should, you're still the only one who has been consistently with both Teaspoon and I for many years."

"He's right," added Click, "if anyone knows these two, it's you."

Emma nervously straightened her glasses and pressed tighter the bun on the back of her brown hair. "Not really," she started to say.

"Click's right," interrupted Michael. "Now out with it."

Emma paused, then set her clipboard down on the table. "I think," she slowly said, "that you should do what you want to do."

"What kind of an answer is that," piped Click.

"Wait a minute," Michael said, "maybe there's more to her answer than first meets the ear."

"What do you mean?"

"I mean, I think what Emma is really saying is that I should do what is right, regardless of whether it's financially beneficial."

"Right-smite," rumbled Click. "I didn't bring you along promoting your career day and night since you were fourteen just to have you turn down a rock and roll opportunity of a lifetime, something any self-respecting basset would give his right thumb for."

"We're not talking music here," replied Michael.

"Of course, we're not," yelled Click. "We're talking politics; and just what do you know about politics?"

"Nothing, I guess," replied Michael.

"Of course, you don't," Click said, "that's why you got me. I'm the one who makes the deals, strikes the business, brings your art to the public. So why don't you listen to me and stay out of my end of the business."

"Because he can't," Emma replied. "That's the plain truth, isn't it, Michael?"

Michael looked at Emma, and for the first time saw her green eyes.

"No, I guess, I can't."

"And why the hell not?" shouted Click.

"Because it involves friendship," said Emma, "something you know little about. While your world is money, his is art. It's that simple. Teaspoon Typhoon stays, or no deal."

It had been the first time that Michael Molecule and the universe's greatest rock promoter had ever disagreed.

"Then I guess there's no more to talk about," said Click. "The deal's off."

"I guess so," Michael replied, then he escorted Emma back to his space pod, where he told Teaspoon to chart a course for home.

* * * * * * * * * *

When Emma left the office after she and Michael had returned and taken the shuttle pod home to her apartment on the west side, she went directly to her telephone and called Harry Sloan, Click Dark's promo man. Sloan and Emma had met on a few occasions: Michael's first album's debut after his release from the army, and more recently they had posed together for the press at Big Star Enterprise's request to promote the last cord concert of the universe. Other than that, Emma hardly knew the man, but she felt compelled to call Sloan under the circumstances.

Sloan was still in his hotel room across the street from Big Star Headquarters, something that Click Dark had related to her at their meeting in the Lyra Lounge on Cygnus. So, it didn't take Emma long to figure out, that by calling him, she might learn the details of why Big Star had backed out on the one chord concert. She needed to know more about why they felt Michael's friendship with Teaspoon was suddenly such a big deal now that both parties, Big Star and Molecule Incorporated, were ready to strike the deal of their corporate lifetimes. Michael's friendship with Teaspoon Typhoon, the robotan, had been no secret, and just about everybody delighted in Teaspoon's intellect and wit. Being one of the very first robotans made before the shortage of Neutrolite had put him by everyone's standards in a class by himself. So, Emma's curiosity got the best of her when Click Dark had related that according to his man Harry Sloan, Michael's friendship with Teaspoon was now the sole impediment to striking a deal.

"Hello."

"Hello, Harry. This is Emma Stark, Michael Molecule's secretary. Could we meet for lunch?"

"Why?"

"To discuss Michael's concert deal with Big Star and why it has lapsed."

"That's pretty clear to everyone," said Sloan.

"I can't help but think that there's more to it," said Emma in a business-like manner.

"As far as I'm concerned, there isn't."

"I can't believe that so many investors would suddenly agree that Michael hangs around with the wrong crowd."

"Business is like that," continued Sloan.

"But it has nothing to do with music."

"Of course not," he continued, "it's promotion and sales. You should know that."

Emma thought for a moment, held the receiver away from her ear. She knew there had to be some way to learn why Teaspoon's acquaintance with Michael had suddenly become so important to so many of the right people.

"But don't you think it's a little odd," continued Emma, "that so many people would rally behind what most had deemed at best a minor issue."

Sloan paused, took a drag on his Regulus cigarette, then mused, "it is a little odd."

"I think," Emma said, "that somebody mounted a little promo campaign themselves among the stockholders to put the nix on the deal."

There was silence from Sloan's end of the line.

"I think we'd better talk," Emma continued. "Meet me at the Leo Minor Café, on Hydra Street at 1:30 pm. And for your sake, you better not be late."

* * * * * * * * * *

While Emma and Harry Sloan prepared to meet for lunch, Michael Molecule was lying on the sofa in his arboretum wondering why the concert had gone wrong. Above him, the globe of glass arched its back like a cat towards the endless blue sky of early afternoon. Michael was sipping from his favorite cup of tea, Vega Erightness, when suddenly his thoughts and privacy were interrupted by a knock at the door. It was Teaspoon, who after securing the spacecraft on the pod back at Molecule's office, had driven his Spectral Sports Car towards Michael's apartment as fast as he could drive.

"Teaspoon, what a surprise," said Michael, as the doors to his exclusive suite slid open and revealed the robotan. "Is something wrong?"

"I'm not sure," replied Teaspoon, his emerald eyes flashing with excitement. "I just heard about the postponement of the Last Chord Concert. What's the problem?"

"The problem is Big Star," said Michael, motioning Teaspoon to have a seat.

"Do they want a larger share of the gate?"

"Nothing like that," Michael said, thinking about how to approach the problem that created the concert's postponement. "It was more of a personal decision on their part."

"What do you mean personal decision?" asked Teaspoon, taking a seat. "Corporations don't have souls and moral obligations."

"They do when it suits their purpose," replied Michael.

"What do you mean?" asked Teaspoon, squinting.

"I mean they simply don't like some of my personal habits. So, they cancelled."

"Ah, come on," said Teaspoon, crossing his arms across his broad chest. "I could see them saying that about the McBison Brothers for sniffing too many Space Blasters before performing. But you?"

"It's less my personal habits," replied Michael, stalling and hoping Teaspoon would not press the issue further, "and more of one relating to the friendships I keep."

"Who don't they like? Emma?"

"No, it isn't her they object to."

"Then who is it?" Teaspoon asked.

"It's you," Michael stated, his voice fading.

"Me!" said Teaspoon. "What the hell do I have to do with anything. I'm just the pilot who flies you around the heavens."

"According to them," said Michael, "you're more than that. You're also a —"

"—Robotan?" asked Teaspoon.

"Exactly," Michael replied, "and the majority of Big Star's stockholders is comprised of a consortium from Altair; and you know what bigots they are."

"Yeah," replied Teaspoon. "I thought that would change after the War of the Windless, that somehow my helping to protect them from a Zenith invasion of Castor and Serius would mean something. But I guess not."

"Yeah, I guess not," replied Michael, "because now it's those same people who are calling our friendship unordinary."

"The only thing that's unordinary about it is that I happened to be a robotan."

Michael looked into Teaspoon's emerald eyes, and saw tears clouding his vision.

"Don't worry," said Michael, getting up and placing a hand on his friend's shoulder. "I just won't perform; call their bluff, and they'll feel it at the bank."

"But this last chord concert means so much to you," Teaspoon replied, looking up.

"Not as much as our friendship."

"Isn't there another way?" asked Teaspoon.

"What do you mean?"

"I mean," continued Teaspoon, suddenly standing up. "Isn't there a way that we can remain friends and the concert could still go on?"

"I doubt it," replied Michael. "Convincing the bigots of Altair to see anything beyond the end of their noses is just about impossible."

"But what if we didn't have to convince them of anything?"

"What do you mean?" asked Michael, as Teaspoon suddenly bolted for the door. "Never mind," Teaspoon said as the door started to slam behind him. "I'll take care of everything. Then the door slammed, and he was gone.

* * * * * * * * * *

When Harry Sloan wasn't being the promo/public relations man for Click Dark, he was seeking out other deals in the universe that would make him money. Not particularly a trustworthy man, one whose loyalty could be counted on, he often told Click Dark that he was working on the promotion of the Big Star deal for Michael Molecule when he wasn't. He didn't consider it a breach of honor, although others were wise to Sloan's excursions into moonlighting, and Emma knew when she sat down with him at the Leo Minor Café that he couldn't be trusted.

"Want a Space Blaster?" Sloan asked, even before Emma was seated at a table located on a veranda.

"Maybe a small one," Emma replied, remembering the importance of her business with Sloan, yet wanting to remain cordial with him.

"So, what do I owe the privilege of your company. I hardly think I have anymore to add to what I've already told you over the phone."

"Some things are better off not discussed over the phone," Emma replied, hoping that Sloan would open up to her.

"If you're looking for some inside negotiating information, you can forget it. I don't spill confidential details given in the privacy of boardroom negotiations."

"Right," replied Emma sarcastically. "Like you never leaked to the press Click Dark's impending signing of the McBison Brothers to a universe contract after Michael strummed the last rock and roll chord at his concert."

"I honestly don't know how the press got that information. They certainly didn't get it from me."

"Get serious, Harry," Emma replied, taking a sip of her Space Blaster brought by the waitress, "everybody in the music business, including me, the press, knows how you work. Your word is as good as a Black Hole, and most people resent that. How Click Dark has put up with your antics for this long is beyond me. I'm not one of your Red Giant beauties from Pollus, so you can cut the con."

Emma watched Sloan squirm in his seat and take a huge snort from his Space Blaster. She was proud of her assertiveness, and she wanted to set him straight to her intentions right away.

"So, tell me. It wasn't really Michael's friendship with Teaspoon Typhoon, the robotan. Was it?"

"Why should I tell you anything," Sloan said, adjusting his necktie to square the knot with the brown of his suit.

"Because if you don't," said Emma, "I'm going to dig until I find out anyway. And if you know what's good for you, you'll get yourself out of this mess before you get yourself in too deep. Now what's really going on?"

Sloan picked up his Space Blaster glass and snorted its contents until only one last vapor remained. He set the glass down on the table and held up his hand for the waitress to bring him another one.

"Okay, Okay," he finally said. "My sources tell me Michael's friendship with Teaspoon was only part of it."

"Which part?" asked Emma. "The big part, or the little?"

"Actually," said Sloan, "his friendship with Teaspoon didn't mean much at all. A couple of the board members mentioned it, and the others followed suit, expressing their desire for Michael to at least cool his friendship with the robotan."

"And what made that vote so easy?"

Sloan hesitated, then leaned forward across the table. His brown eyes narrowed in confidentiality.

"It was Click Dark," said Sloan, "he's the one who greased the vote." "Why would he do that?" asked Emma, "He's got more to lose if Michael doesn't perform than anybody."

"He says he does," stated Sloan, "but actually he can expect to lose a bundle if Molecule puts an end to rock and roll. Frankly, the news I leaked to the public through the press about Click's new sensation, the McBison Brothers, wasn't exactly met with a consensus agreement."

"You mean, the McBison Brothers are not going to be the hit that Dark thought, despite all of the planned promotion?"

"That's right," Sloan replied, easing back into his seat. "They're a couple of no-talent fools who love Space Blasters more than they love making music."

"So, Click would just as soon not put an end to rock and roll, after all?"

"That's right. If he does, he stands to lose billions."

* * * * * * * * * *

While Sloan told Emma about all of the details concerning Click Dark's promotion of, yet sabotaging of Michael's attempt to put an end to rock and roll by playing the last chord at a rock quarry on an Orion hillside, it was to this hillside that Teaspoon traveled after his conversation with Michael. At the moment, Teaspoon was confused by the bigotry. Over the years the confusion had not lessened, but he figured there was more to the whole business than that. So he had flown to Orion to speak to Pinkus, the chief roadie in charge of stage and sound for the concert, and found him with all 10,000 members of his crew, local 2300 of the musicians' union, sitting down at the concert site, awaiting further orders. Pinkus recognized Michael Molecule's famous robotan friend and stood up from a seated position on the shale hillside to shake his hand.

"Teaspoon Typhoon?"

"That's right," replied Teaspoon.

"What's going on?" asked Pinkus. "We haven't heard the reason for the concert's cancellation."

"It was cancelled because of my friendship with Michael."

"That cuts me to the quick," said Pinkus.

"And if you don't set up the concert site," replied Teaspoon, "you'll be helping their cause. The best thing you could do would be to set up the concert equipment and hope that Molecule will play."

"Do you think he will?"

"Yes," Teaspoon replied.

"But what about the money?" Pinkus asked. "Surely you can't expect him to play for nothing?"

"I do," Teaspoon said, "if I can count on you to get your robotans to set the stage without pay."

"I don't know," Pinkus said. "A lot of these robotans haven't worked in years, some are even working for the first time, fresh from the ghettos of Gazelle."

"I know, I know," said Teaspoon, "but what do we have if we let the universe think that a handful of corporate bigots can tell us what to do?"

"Not much," replied Pinkus.

"So, will you help me?"

"I'll do what I can," Pinkus said, "but I can't guarantee a hundred percent. Some of these robotans are pretty hungry and working for nothing won't be very appetizing."

* * * * * * * * * *

While Teaspoon was convincing Pinkus to rally his roadies to set up the concert site for Michael's Last Chord Concert, Michael, unnerved by Teaspoon's abrupt exit from his office, went to see Click Dark. Click was in his office dictating a letter. Michael arrived a short time after Click had started his dialogue with his speech-in-nod machine, and hearing his voice, Michael stopped at Click's office door, thinking that Click had someone inside. Click never used a secretary; he said he didn't trust them, or anyone, except his promo man Sloan; and for this reason, Michael should have suspected Click was alone. But the thought didn't occur to him, and he stood waiting for Click's conversation to end with what would turn out to be a phantom client.

"The cancellation of Michael Molecule's concert," Click's voice said behind his door, "is because the promotion of the McBison Brothers has not established their popularity, and the public's reception of the O-Zone Chute. The Board of Directors, under my advisement, has decided to temporarily cancel the Last Chord Concert until the McBison Brothers' popularity is substantiated to warrant a universe tour. Michael Molecule's friendship to his robotan pilot, Teaspoon Typhoon, although of minor importance, has been used to mask our public relations error in regards to the McBisons and the underestimating of the universe's love for rock and roll. Until such time that it can be re-scheduled, the concert has been cancelled under the guise of racial prejudice. It will, however, be re-scheduled at the proper time, when the business climate is suitable. Sincerely yours, Click Dark."

Outside the door, Michael could hardly believe his ears, and his first inclination was to charge into Click's office and confront him. But then, he began to think in larger, more universal dimensions, and he quickly and quietly left.

CHAPTER TWO

Emma went straight to Michael's apartment after her meeting at the Leo Minor Café with Sloan. There, she found him standing under the huge glass dome, tuning his guitar. His back was to her, and she had, in her haste, entered without knocking, something a few hours ago she would have never done. But now, after learning of the real reason behind the concert's cancellation, she felt closer to Michael than she had ever felt before. At first, Michael just felt Emma's hand on his shoulder, and then he turned to see her as he had never seen her before. Her face was flushed, as if she had been running all afternoon. Beyond that, Michael noticed that her hair was messy, undone from its usual tight-knotted bun. Loose, curling strands of brown hair now hung about Emma's shoulders. Michael, struck by her beauty, unbuckled his strap and set down his guitar. Then he stood looking into Emma's deep green eyes.

"You found out, didn't you?" Michael said grasping one of her hands.

"Yes," Emma replied. "Sloan told me everything. But how do you know?"

"I went to see Click, and overheard him talking to his speech-in-nod machine. Isn't it ironic," said Michael, "that Click's distrust of almost everyone has cost him the public's knowledge of the greatest promotional ploy of his life. Yet, there's not much we can do about it."

"What do you mean?" Emma asked.

"We're stuck," said Michael, "at the mercy of the promo men. I'd give the concert and support my friends, yet no one would get paid. Beyond that, if I give it, I end rock and roll forever, and now I'm not sure I want to do that."

"You're forgetting another thing," Emma said.

"What's that?"

"You couldn't give the concert even if you wanted to. Click has probably discontinued the sound stage and equipment set-up."

"He did," replied another voice suddenly entering the room. Michael and Emma turned to see Teaspoon Typhoon. "But I continued it. I've been over to Orion talking to Pinkus and the other sound technicians, and they've agreed to set the stage for the Last Chord Concert, with or without pay. It seems they didn't think much of the bigots from Altain on Big Star's Board of Directors."

"But there's much more involved in the concert's cancellation than that," said Michael.

"That's right," added Emma.

"I suppose there is," Teaspoon replied, "and you both can tell me all about it while I fly you both out to Orion for the Last Chord Concert. Michael, are you sure you want to end rock and roll?"

"I don't know," Michael replied. "I guess I'll find that out when I get there."

Then they left the earth behind them and headed for interstellar space in Cosmos IV with Teaspoon at the helm.

* * * * * * * * * *

After years of being in the rock and roll business, it didn't take Click Dark long to figure out what Michael, Emma, and Teaspoon were up to. Harry Sloan, who always played both sides of the net, had told him everything, soon after his Leo Minor Café meeting with Emma. Harry, a businessman, had gone straight to Dark's office to tell him how he had "spelled the beans" to Emma.

"You've always talked too much," Click Dark had replied, then he shoved Harry Sloan into his space pod and made for Orion, where he hoped to stop the Last Chord Concert until the promotional time was right.

* * * * * * * * *

Teaspoon Typhoon, the robotan pilot, eased Michael's executive Cosmos IV to a halt next to the concert site, and as their Cosmos IV's doors opened, they were met by a beaming Pinkus, who with the help of all of the robotan roadies had prepared the site for the concert. Pinkus and his men had used gamma ray jack hammers and anti-matter chisels to break down the hydrogen atoms in the rock face of two cliffs; and after hauling away the rubble, had liberated protons and electrons to heat a steady-state theory to implant Three Leap Speakers eighty stories high.

"Wow," gasped Michael, as soon as he had stepped out of the space pod.

"Well, you are going to play the universe with the last chord of rock and roll," said Pinkus. "The roadies and I wanted it to be a good jam."

"Thank you," said Michael, shaking the burly robotan's hand. "I'll do my best."

Michael, Teaspoon, and Emma walked over to the four-story stage. "How do we get up there?" Emma asked.

"The elevator," replied Pinkus, following behind them. "It's located in the middle, under the stage. Good luck," he added, turning to leave. "It's time for me to rejoin my friends in the bleachers." Then Pinkus, the robotan who would later become known as the Premiere Roadie, waved.

"Thanks again," Michael called out to him.

"The pleasure was all mine," Pinkus yelled back. "Now I've got something to tell my grandchildren."

"Tell them it was the best one chord concert you ever heard."

"I'll tell them," shouted Pinkus. Then he was gone.

"This is where I part company, too," Teaspoon said.

"Only for a little while, I hope," said Michael.

"If you say so, boss," came Teaspoon's reply. Then he, too, disappeared.

"Come with me, Emma," Michael suddenly said, grabbing Emma's hand.

"If you say so, boss," she replied, mocking Teaspoon's reply.

"I say so," Michael replied. "We've got a one chord concert to play."

Emma stayed next to Michael and ascended with him in the elevator up to the concert stage's fourth story platform. There, the elevator clicked to a halt, its top flush with the platform, and Michael and Emma made their way carefully through a series of steel catwalks that brought them eventually to center stage. When they appeared, a tremendous thunder of applause from 10,000 robotan roadies filled the air of the quarry, and Michael took Emma's hand in his, and raised both of their hands together above their heads. His gesture was met with thunderous approval, and when their hands were lowered, Michael and Emma looked into each other's eyes, his blue vision meeting her green, in what seemed like an eternity for both of them. Then they kissed, and around them heard the sounds of exploding galaxies rushing from the crowd as they voiced their approval. Emma then quickly slipped away to one side of center stage, leaving the blond-haired Michael alone, guitar strapped over one shoulder. Suddenly, all was silent, like the mass of the universe had been brought to a sudden standstill, the kinetic energy halting in every atom. Michael, sensing the magnetic force pulling him deeper into a magnetic field, placed his fingers in a "G" chord position on the frets of the guitar. Position one. For the slow handed. Then he pinched his gold pic between his two experienced fingers; it's glittering light signaling towards the darkness beyond them in the universe. Then with a raised hand and crooked elbow, he quickly lowered his hand and arm in a powerful downward momentum, striking the pic across the strings in a perfect "G". And there was nothing that Click Dark could do about it, except maybe listen to its clarity from miles away in space.

CHAPTER THREE

When Click Dark heard the last chord of rock and roll, as strummed by Michael Molecule at the Last Chord Concert on Orion, he instructed his pilot, a robotan named Lilly, to land on Corona, only a few light years away. He knew that continuing onto Orion to stop the Last Chord Concert was now a lost cause, so as Lilly veered left away from the original destination of Orion, Click knew he had to think fast. Music, rock and roll had been Click's life; the only thing he knew for sure, that and the fact that Corona Borealis was where the McBison Brothers, the O-Zone Chute duo, often held up between concert gigs. The McBisons, Phil and Don, owned a small villa on the north shore of the Serpent's Sea; and from there, they drank triple atom Space Blasters until they couldn't walk, and practiced their O-Zone Chutes.

Their villa had orange tiled roofs, much like the earth's Mediterranean architecture, and white Spanish stucco walls from a similar earth design. The north face of the villa was glass and faced the Serpen's Sea and the Virgo Mountains that loomed behind it. When Click Dark's space pod landed, it did so on the northeast side of the villa, on a landing pod designed to accommodate the largest of space buses. Click, like Michael Molecule, owned a Cosmos IV, and when he and Lilly stepped out of the pod, the stairs extending down in front of them, the McBison Brothers watched their every move from inside their glass enclosure. They had seen Click's space pod approaching from a distance, just a silver speck against the darkness of space over the mountains and had commented to each other about the oddity of the visit. The McBison Brothers received few visitors, and in their privacy had sought to buffer themselves against their increasing popularity among the universe's O-Zone Chute lovers, but they had not opted to hire guard dogs or erect proton fences, given the remote proximity of their estate from the mainstream universe. So, it was with casual curiosity that the McBisons watched Click Dark's space pod approach, only to see him and his pilot descend the steps and cross the rock lawn to knock at their door.

Phil McBison, the older and larger of the two brothers, got up from his seated position from behind a Bootes Grand Piano, and made his way across the living room to answer the door, while Don McBison remained seated, staring at his Space Blaster, his fourth of the afternoon.

"Click," said Phil McBison, upon answering the door. "What brings you out to Corona Borealis?"

"Business, as usual," Click replied. "Due to a strange turn of events, I've had to move forward the date of your O-Zone Chute tour of the universe."

"I thought that was all decided," said Don McBison, hearing the conversation and standing.

"It was," Click replied, "but that meddling Michael Molecule spoiled our plans by putting his time-honored decency above money."

"You mean he played the Last Chord Concert, despite the threat of Big Star Enterprises pulling out of the deal?"

"Not only did he play," said Click, "but he convinced Pinkus and the other robotan roadies to set up the sound stage and equipment to the max, despite not being paid for it."

"He must be some kind of guy," said Phil.

"Was some kind of guy," corrected Click. "With the expected playing of his last chord comes the demise of rock and roll in the universe, and now it's up to us—that is, you—to carry on the universe's music tradition."

"I don't know," said Phil, closing the door behind Click and Lilly, and motioning them to take a seat. "That wasn't our original deal."

"I know," Click said, taking a seat, with Lilly next to him, "but like I say our plans have changed. They've been moved up."

"And just when I was getting comfortable with the old plan," Phil said, once again taking a seat behind his piano.

The original plan devised by Click Dark for the McBison Brother's universe promotion was for them to live on Corona Borealis for awhile until their absence on the music scene either spawned a greater appreciation of the O-Zone Chute, or until Michael Molecule had worn out rock and roll and played its last chord. But things had not gone according to plan. The universe didn't tire of rock and roll as easily as Click and his promoters had anticipated, and Molecule, despite its resilient popularity, was going to put an end to it anyway with his last chord concert to spite the money-changers and bigots.

"I can't believe that Molecule would do such a thing," Click stated, watching Don sit down across from him.

"You couldn't have foreseen it," Don replied. "Who would have thought that in this day and age of rock and roll that one would still have a thread of honesty."

"Yeah, don't take it so hard," added Phil, pounding a few notes on the piano, "you'll find working with us much easier."

Over the years, the McBison Brothers had earned the reputation of being the bad boys of the music industry. Always dressed in dark sweaters and tight telescope pants, their black hair long and greasy, they had broken up nearly every piece of furniture in every club they had ever played in from Epsilon to Ursa Minor. And if they weren't personally breaking up the furniture, their music, at first perceived as mello, incited people to violence and they broke up the furniture, and therein laid the secret to their growing popularity. While their appearance was black leather and raunchy, their music was seemingly harmless, that is until it imbedded itself clearly in your mind. Then, the so-called soft sounds of the O-Zone Chute, air pushed through reeds of straw, produced a violent effect. Some scientists on Alpha Apus had a been experimenting with the physical and emotional effects of the McBison Brothers' music. One scientist, Dr. Spry Algol, even went so far as to say in an article in <u>Universe Tonight</u> that O-Zone Chute music should be banned because of its potential hazard to mind control by eliciting the worst possible behavior in its listeners.

"The high-pitched melody," wrote scientist Algol, "is actually very deceiving. On one hand, the listener is lulled into a passive state, while on the other his subconscious is incited to violent behavior. The McBison's music should be banned until further Alpha tests can prove it either harmful or harmless."

Of course, Click Dark had loved Professor Algol's article, because as a promoter of rock and roll he knew that the more harmful something is for people, especially adolescents, the more they want of it. So right after Algol's article had appeared in <u>Universe Tonight Magazine</u> several years ago, Click had started to promote the McBisons and Michael Molecule with equal fever, hoping that when Molecule and rock and roll ended, that the new O-Zone Chute music of the McBison Brothers would take up the slack. But things, as Click had explained on arriving at the McBison's villa, hadn't gone according to plan, and the demise of rock and roll had come too soon, and the McBisons were about to be thrust into the universe's limelite earlier than they thought, despite their protest.

"But I was just getting settled into our first plan of action," Don said, getting up from a chair to mix himself another Space Blaster from a bar not far from where Click and Lilly were seated.

"You mean, you were just working up your tolerance for 12 Space Blasters a day," Phil said, running his fingers nervously along the piano keys, an arpeggio filling the air.

"You've got nothing much to talk about," said Don. "For a while there, you were hitting the Blasters pretty heavily, too."

"That's until I found out that music was more important than getting silly all the time snorting three atoms."

"My, my," Don replied, "you sound a bit like Michael Molecule. Wasn't he the one who said, 'Art's my life; I don't give a damn about nothing else?'"

"That's right," said Click, "that was one lyric from <u>January 15, A Song About Capricorn Rising</u>."

"No," interrupted Lilly, "that was a lyric from Molecule's earlier version of <u>Scorpus</u>."

"To listen to you two talk," said Don, carrying his newly prepared Space Blaster back to his seat, "it sounds like it's Molecule and not us who has the future of the universe's music in his hands."

"We're sorry," Click said, regaining his business composure. "You're right, Don. The future of the musical universe is now in yours and Phil's hands. Molecule gave us the in-roads; now it's the O-Zone Chutes melodies turn to plow us the highways."

* * * * * * * * * *

Dr. Artemus Algol, the scientist from Alpha Apus, who had been studying the effects of the sounds of the O-Zone Chute's music on both humans and robotans, had only concluded this morning the definitive study that would clearly indicate that the octave and frequency of the O-Zone Chute was hazardous. And as Click and Lilly met with the McBison Brothers on Corona Borealis to discuss how to gear up the McBison's universe concert and popularity, Dr. Algol was just coming out of his laboratory on Alpha Apus. Algol had long white hair and a long pointed nose, and always wore a white laboratory smock, no matter what the occasion. A former research chemist in bio-feedback electron energy at Gemini University, in his later years he had shunned the academic life for private research and had built himself a musical/ scientific laboratory close to his house. Every day at noon, Dr. Algol walked from his lab to his house for lunch and left behind in his lab the most sophisticated tuning devices in the universe. Sitting on the lab counter, just inside the door, was the Ecliptic Process Midline, a solar root that measured the impact of musical variation on brain waves. And just to the left of it, Algol had made his own Libra Julian Scale, a calibrated weight measurement designed to actually weigh the consequences of the musical impact in terms of psychological duress, as they are associated with prior experience. For his research on the effects of the O-Zone Chute, Dr. Algol had used his lab assistant, Henry Otter, a slight lad of 25, whose thick obtrusive eyeglasses almost made him blind. Dr. Algol had long ago concluded that Henry, although not brilliant, was smart enough to comprehend the experiments made on him and respond to Algol's questions accurately.

Henry Otter, before he had been a research scientist studying with Dr. Algol at Gemini University, compliments of a Pisces Scholarship from the Music Institute of the Universe, had actually traveled for awhile as the back-up bass player for Michael Molecule, when he played the smaller clubs in deeper space. Molecule didn't like to transport his own band "The Rocket Launchers" to places like Ophinchus because it was too costly, so he relied on Click Dark's judgement to book him suitable replacements when he traveled that far out into the universe. And Henry Otter had been happy playing Bass for Molecule, who every so often made the rounds of the outer universe, because he liked the closeness of the fans.

Most of the clubs where Henry Otter had played back-up bass for Molecule had been small. There was The Great Bear Club on the Big Dipper and The Guard Stars Club nearby on Kocab. No more than a few hundred fans could be jammed into either of the clubs at any one time. The scientist hadn't gotten a chance to know Michael Molecule, and it had saddened him when while standing in the lab, he and Dr. Algol had heard a tremendous G chord being strummed from the heavens.

"That must be it," Dr. Algol had said to him, as soon as the vibration from the G chord had stopped shaking the lab.

"Must be what?" Henry had asked.

"The last chord of rock and roll," Algol had replied.

"What makes you think so?"

"It was bound to be played," said Algol. "It was only a matter of time."

While Dr. Algol attached the sensory wires to Henry's chest and skull, Henry's thoughts took him back to when he was an undergraduate student at Gemini University. Back then, he thought, momentarily helping Dr. Algol attach a wire to his arm, he couldn't walk on a sidewalk passed a dormitory without hearing the rock lyrics of Molecule's Phroton Albums. "Northern celestial light," Henry heard ring in his ears, "bring back the religion of life to me."

Boy, thought Henry, feeling Dr. Algol's fingertips adjusting the last wire, that was music.

"Are you ready?" asked Dr. Algol, suddenly stepping back, and walking over to a nearby wall switch.

"Ready as I ever am," Henry stated flatly.

"Buck-up," replied the professor, "this is the last experiment on the effects of the O-Zone Chute on the mental stability of people. In a moment, it will be all over, and you'll be as good as new."

"What about for now," explained Henry.

"For now," said Professor Algol, "you'll just have to endure." Then he threw the switch.

* * * * * * * * *

When Pinkus, the Chief roady of Michael Molecule's Last Chord Concert, heard Michael strum rock and roll's last chord, and then saw

Molecule's space pod disappear into the blackness of space, with Michael and Emma, his secretary in it, Pinkus knew that a dark time for robotan roadies was coming. No more could robotans from the ghettos of Gazelle depend on music for work. With the Last Chord Concert came the death of rock and roll, and with it, Pinkus thought while leaving his bleacher seat at the concert on Orion, came hard times for robotans everywhere. Ever since the interstellar police had regulated his roadies activities at concert sites, Pinkus had seen the time coming when his job would be consumed by technology and the greed of human beings. One way or the other, Pinkus had seen the robotan's role in the evolution of universe music slowly decreasing. And now with the pre-mature death of rock and roll, millions of robotan roadies would be out of work.

When Pinkus left the concert site and climbed into his old, beat-up space pod, a Cluster I, the thought of his uncertain future was coupled by another. It was hard enough trying to live with Colonel Status of the interstellar police when he was employed. But now, with rock and roll gone he, while having survived its death with dignity, was—nevertheless—now unemployed, and Status would be gunning for him.

John Pinkus, the chief roady of all roadies, had been a scientific mistake when he was built at the Robotan Plant on Pegasus by the Polaris Company. Much like Teaspoon Typhoon, Michael Molecule's robotan pilot, Pinkus had been a product of early robotan design. And while he certainly did not have the intellect or wit of Teaspoon, he was without a doubt more intellectual than others of his kind. So, as he flew home from the Last Chord Concert to Merack, alone and bored, in his Cluster Space Pod I, his thoughts were not only for himself, but for all other robotans who had been roadies, and now faced similar unemployment. It was true, he thought, easing his space pod onto the parking lot pod outside of the Mercury Apartments, where he lived, that many robotans, despite the end of rock and roll would still be gainfully employed. But as he thought about their work, it became clear that only music offered the robotan a bright and rewarding future beyond servitude, for most robotans were still working in low-paying jobs. Yet, almost none were musicians, and now that rock and roll was closed, there would even be fewer and fewer musicians playing in the small clubs in and around the ghettos of Gazelle. By the time Pinkus reached his front door, he knew that he wouldn't be staying in his apartment for long. For the longer he sat in it thinking, the less likely he would be to do something to help himself and his robotan friends.

* * * * * * * * * *

Phil McBison, the piano playing brother of Don, finally stood up from the piano and made himself a Space Blaster.

"Would you like one?" he asked Click Dark, and his robotan pilot Lilly, who were still seated in his living room.

"See what did I tell you about Phil's hypocrisy when it comes to secretly hitting the Space Blasters. All along, he tells other people how much I snort, and he does just as much."

"No thanks," Click replied, interrupting Don's tirade.

"Me either," Lilly said.

With that, Phil proceeded to make himself a triple atom.

"You both better go easy on the Space Blasters," said Click. "We've got some serious business to discuss, and not much time to discuss it."

"What do you mean?" Don asked.

"First of all," said Click, glancing at Lilly, "we've got to move forward with the O-Zone Chute Universe tour. Molecule by ending rock and roll with the Last Chord Concert has left us no choice. Second, we've got to fight the accusations of that crack pot Professor Algol from Alpha Apus whose research is proving that O-Zone Chute music is harmful to people."

"Of course, it is," said Phil, taking his Space Blaster and sitting on the floor cross-legged in leather pants, "that's why they like it so much."

"But according to Professor Algol," continued Click, "the octaves from the O-Zone Chute can drive people insane by disrupting brain frequency patterns. That's why listeners like to stand on their heads about half-way through your concerts."

It was true. O-Zone Chute fans who attended the McBison Brothers' concerts could only stand about one-half concert's worth of O-Zone Chute music before they went wild, held their ears, and then stood on their heads for relief, the theory being that blood rushing to their brains helped them to combat the sound.

"So how are we going to fight the accusations of Dr. Algol, when in fact they are true," asked Phil, setting down his Space Blaster on the table.

"For a while, at least," Click replied, "you're going to have to stop your concerts before they stand on their heads, to refute the accusations of Dr. Algol and his scientific experiments."

"And at the same time," asked Don, very much into his fourth Space Blaster, "that you want us to ease up on the audience, you also want us to gain popularity by knocking them out. Just how do you propose to do that?"

"I don't know," Click replied. "But for now the O-Zone Chute is the universe's replacement for rock and roll, and you're the only act I got with impending star status, so let's try to work together on the promotion of this so we can both survive."

"Survival at half speed is not my nature," replied Don, guzzling what was left of his fourth Space Blaster.

"Talk to him, Phil. Will ya?" said Click. "I've got you booked into Mercury's Strata Lounge tonight?"

"So soon?" Phil replied.

"We can't let the Professor's accusations gain too much momentum. That's why we have to get you in front of an audience as soon as possible to prove that your O-Zone Chute music does not do what Professor Algol says it does. Be at the concert site at 8 p.m. And for Cletus Sake, stop snorting so much."

* * * * * * * * * *

When Professor Algol, the scientist testing the effects of O-Zone Chute music on brain wave dysfunction, threw the switch hooked to the electrode monitors wired to Henry Otter, his assistant's body, Henry at first did nothing. Then his brown eyes went blank, and they started to twirl in their sockets, normal behavior according to an earlier article written about the effects of O-Zone Chute music by Dr. Swingline in <u>SuperNova</u>. But after one hour, Henry's eyes stopped twirling; his feet started moving involuntarily, and his fingers started snapping a complicated rhythm. Dr. Algol's experiments on his assistant Henry had substantiated that Henry's finger snapping and toe tapping behavior were the first mutant signs that his guinea pig was beginning to become involved by the rhythmic melody of the O-Zone Chute. Then suddenly, in every experiment to date, Dr. Algol had recorded that following a period of dancing, first slow then more and more rapid, the listener started jumping uncontrollably, trying to reverse his body position. In short, his legs became his brain, and his brain his legs, with the sudden impulses in his legs eventually taking over and over-riding his brain's message to remain erect. Then, in one swift motion, the dancing ceased, and the listener, in this case Henry, leaped into the air, landing on the floor on the top of his head, where he remained in quiet contemplation. It was this state of subconsciousness that Dr. Algol alluded to as harmful; therefore, he sought conclusive evidence to present to the Word Order of Musical Interpretation, who regularly published the universe's Top 100 hits.

When Dr. Algol left his lab that day for lunch, notebook under arm with his conclusive findings, he had left Henry, his assistant, as he always had, standing on his head on the floor in the middle of his lab. But when he left today, he had a huge smile on his face, for today he was both finished with his experiment and with Henry, who he regarded as a potential threat to his being the sole recipient of the Slammy Awards for Music.

* * * * * * * * * *

When Pinkus, the Intergalactic roadie for Michael Molecule, had parked his old space pod, Cluster I, and had walked the length of the tubeway and entered his apartment, he placed a call to Click Dark's office. There, the telephone rang thirty times, until Click Dark finally answered it, having just been piloted back from the McBison Brothers' villa on Corona Borealis.

"Hello."

"What took you so long?"

"Who is this?"

"This is Pinkus, the universe's chief roadie."

"You mean, the ex-chief roadie," Click replied.

"Get serious," Pinkus said. "Business is business."

"That's right," Click replied. "And what you did by setting up the Molecule Last Chord Concert without pay was bad business."

"It might have been bad business, but the fact is, you still need me if the McBison Brothers are going to play tonight."

"How did you know about the McBison's gig tonight at Mercury's Strata Lounge?"

"I didn't," Pinkus replied, "not until you just told me, but I figured you'd have the McBisons playing their little hearts out as soon as possible, especially with the bad publicity surrounding Dr. Algol's O-Zone Chute experiments, which brings us to the question of using me and my roadies for all of McBison's gigs."

"You've got to be kidding," Click replied. "The simple truth is that I can't trust you."

"And I can't trust you either," said Pinkus. "But both of us have no choice. You need your McBison concerts to be as clean as possible, and me and my roadie robotans need work."

Click Dark thought for a moment. But his pause at the other end of the line was more for effect than for threat. Pinkus, on the line's other end, knew that Click couldn't make a move without his robotan roadies, something that he had hoped Click had realized too.

"I could always hire non-union robotans," Click said.

"At this late date," Pinkus replied. "Don't be silly; you've got to get the McBison's universe tour off the ground by tonight."

It was true, Click thought. He needed Pinkus' help.

"Okay," Click finally said. "Get yourself up there with 2,000 roadies. And make the sound in Mercury's Strata Lounge universe long."

"Gottcha," Pinkus replied, then hung up the phone.

Pinkus' telephone wasn't even settled in its cradle when he heaved a huge sigh of relief. He had not known for sure about either the McBison Brothers concert tonight, or whether Click Dark had already hired non-union roadies. But his bluff on both accounts had worked, and some of his roadies would keep working despite Michael Molecule's strumming of the last chord of rock and roll.

* * * * * * * * *

When Henry, Dr. Algol's research assistant, finally fell to the floor, the effects of the experiments of the O-Zone Chute finally wearing off, he heard voices outside the lab, and went out to investigate. His head hurt, and he had trouble focusing his eyes, but his ears seemed to hear normally, at least he thought they could, until he made out Dr. Algol's voice coming out an open window of his house.

"Yes, yes, this is Dr. Algol," stated the Professor. "Is this the Department for the Slammy Awards for Music?"

"Yes."

"Good. I'm glad to announce that I have single-handedly found that O-Zone Chute music is definitely dangerous to a listener's health."

"Congratulations," said an anonymous voice on the other end of the line.

"Thank you," said Dr. Algol. "When do you want the results of my experiments?"

"Just a moment," said the voice, "I'll connect you with the right person." There was a strange clicking sound at the other end of the line, and Dr. Algol waited a moment for a better connection. Then suddenly a voice said, "Dr. Algol?"

"Yes," the Dr. replied.

"Tell me of your findings."

"I have conclusive evidence that O-Zone Chute music is hazardous to a listener's health and should be discontinued."

"I see," said the voice.

"To whom am I speaking?" Dr. Algol asked. But instead of an answer, he only heard the click of the receiver on the other end of the line.

CHAPTER FOUR

When Michael Molecule and Emma, his secretary, left the Last Chord Concert site, flown by Teaspoon Typhoon in Michael's Cosmos IV space pod, both Michael and Emma's thoughts were torn. Michael was both happy that he had grown closer to Emma, and had, in fact, played the final chord of rock and roll with her in mind. If he couldn't have rock and roll, his sister and mother of melody, then at least he could have the companionship of Emma, who he had been increasingly aware of since this morning, when the Last Chord Concert was at first cancelled. Relaxing in his space pod, Teaspoon at the helm, and with Emma next to him, Michael knew that his life was taking new directions. He had been feeling that way for weeks; with his music less than it used to be, he knew that a change away from rock and roll was inevitable. And now that Emma was entering his life, he, as he stood on the stage for the last chord concert at Orion, knew that she would replace his fading feeling for music. Yet, despite the replacement of old for new, and the moving forward with his life—out of rock and roll, he couldn't help but feel sorry for the robotan roadies, led by Pinkus, some of whom hadn't worked for years; and thanks to his noble effort of continuing the concert, wouldn't work again.

"What's the matter?" Emma asked, in a concerned voice.

"Nothing."

"Come on," Emma said, "I've seen that painful look before."

"When?" Michael asked, half joking, and grabbing Emma's hand.

"When you've been trying to write music."

"I was just thinking about Pinkus, and the other roadies. Thanks to my last chord of rock and roll, played in the name of social justice, they're unemployed, and may never work again."

"Sure, they will," said Emma. "Pinkus, especially, is too smart to sit around for long. I bet he's already cooked up something for himself and his fellow roadies."

"I hope so," Michael replied. "It was enough playing the last chord concert knowing my life was going into other directions without having the weight of the robotans' fate to carry around as well."

"What new directions?" Emma asked, knowing precisely what Michael was talking about, for her life, as well, had changed dramatically during the past few hours. This morning she had been a timid, but faithful secretary to Michael Molecule, at Molecule Enterprises, and now she was Molecule's confidant and girlfriend, a big leap for Emma, who for years had been a lonely introvert.

"You know," said Michael, "I never could have done it without your help."

"You mean played the last chord?"

"That's right," replied Michael. "It was my future with you that actually committed me to strum it. Before you, I had been a middle of the road attitude, never taking sides, always playing for the money and myself and not much else. But today, I ended rock and roll music not for me, but for the social injustice done to Pinkus and his roadies."

"Come on, you must have played it a little for yourself, knowing that you'd get me?"

"Okay," Michael replied, laughing. "I guess there were other consideration levels involved. But primarily, I did it for someone else. And standing back there on the stage at the Orion with the guitar pic in my hand, I knew that if I strummed the guitar that I, too, would be unemployed. And you know something—it didn't make any difference.

"You'll be talked about for years for what you did," Emma said. "You probably put the universe light years ahead in dealing with its own prejudice."

"I don't know about that," Michael replied modestly. "But I do know that bigots on Altair will think twice now before being so blatantly obvious about their actions. And who knows, maybe the actions will become so remote that they'll forget about them."

"Could be," Emma replied, snuggling closer to Michael, but well aware that it would take more than a single chord strummed in the note of decency before the bigots of Altair, or anywhere else, for that matter, came to their senses.

* * * * * * * * *

When Col. Status of the Interstellar Police heard Michael Molecule's last G chord strummed in the name of decency, he was driving home in an Interstellar Squad Pod, the radio tuned to intergalactic space. At the time he heard the last chord shake the metal form of his space pod, his thoughts ironically were of Pinkus, the universe's chief roadie, for who Col. Status had no love. Pinkus, he thought, was too uppity; his actions were not consistent with the actions of other robotans, and he, Col. Status, had only a few months ago decided to put Pinkus in his robotan place, something Michael Molecule knew nothing about. And now that Pinkus and his roadies were unemployed, Col. Status thought it an opportune time to roust Pinkus, whom he knew lived in the Galaxy Apartments on Magar. Col. Status, a big man, could do it too, something that Pinkus knew, as he watched Status' Lenox space pod land on a pad nearby. Then he heard a knock at the door.

"Well, well," said Col. Status, his brown eyes flashing, and his slender mustache twitching. "How's my little unemployed robotan friend?"

"Just fine," Pinkus replied, keeping his hand on the doorknob. "You'll have to excuse me if I neglect to invite you in."

"Oh, that's okay," Col. Status replied, sticking his thumbs where a black belt met his brown pants, part of the uniform worn by all Interstellar Space Police Troopers. "I wouldn't want to overstay my welcome."

"You have all ready," Pinkus stated. "Did you want anything special?"

"No," Col. Status stated. "I just wanted to see how life was amid the ranks of the unemployed."

"I wouldn't know," Pinkus replied.

"What'll you mean?"

"I mean," continued Pinkus, "I'm not unemployed, although that certainly is none of your business."

When Pinkus said it was none of Col. Status' business, he could see Col. Status clench his fists, for it was exactly talk like that that infuriated Status.

"Of course, your business is my business!" Status yelled. "You robotans have no rights on Magar or anywhere else."

"Maybe," said Pinkus. "But that doesn't give you the right to come over here to check on me."

"Oh no," Status replied, "and just who's going to complain?"

Pinkus knew that as far as arguments go that he was at the end of his, for robotans, as he well knew, not only had no rights, but those who were set free by their owners, like Pinkus had been years ago, also had no one to speak for them. It was common knowledge that a freed robotan was not a free robotan, something Molecule had made mention of in his song <u>2484: Robotans Be Free</u>.

"And where are you working now?" asked Col. Status, taking out a pencil and a notebook to record the information about Pinkus.

"If you want to know so bad," Pinkus replied, "why don't you go down to Intergalactic Space Police Headquarters and check the neutron computer; I just called in my employment change with all of the pertinent data."

"Why don't you save me the trouble," Col. Status replied. "Headquarters is a half a light year away, and I don't feel like walking all the way across your lawn to my space pod to radio in to ask."

Pinkus watched Status release one of his clenched fists and take off his reflector sunglasses, which he stuffed into his shirt pocket, as if expecting trouble.

"Oh, no you don't," Pinkus replied. "You're not going to suck me into doing something stupid this time, once is enough."

The incident referred to by Pinkus had happened up on Mercury outside the Strata Lounge, where Michael Molecule had been playing a three-night gig, supported by the fine sound system as provided for by Pinkus and 3,000 of his roadies. Pinkus had just finished overseeing the installation of the ten story Three Leaps Speaker System and had entered the small control shed that contained the major control for the system: one huge volume knob. Actually, the shed was too small, as Pinkus remembered, standing in his living room doorway talking to Status, so small, in fact, that the one six-foot diameter knob almost extended to rub against the insides of the shed's walls. Pinkus was routinely checking the rotation of the knob for variations in volume when Col. Status had appeared at the door of the shed, his pistol drawn.

"What's going on?" Pinkus had remembered saying.

"Nothing," Status had remarked.

"Then why the drawn laser gun?"

"What drawn laser gun," Status had replied, and then blatantly started shooting holes into the walls around Pinkus, who despite the threat to his life had remained perfectly still.

"Can't be scared, huh?" Status had grunted, upon emptying the chamber of his laser gun into the wall. "Well, let's see how you react to the charge of resisting arrest."

"Resisting arrest," Pinkus replied. "Arrest for what?"

"For operating a sound system without a special robotan permit."

"But I got a permit," Pinkus had responded. "It's right over there."

Pinkus turned and pointed towards the wall, where only this morning he had tacked the square permit. But now, after Status' laser gun spree, the once six-inch square permit was nothing but confetti, which Pinkus, no matter how hard he tried couldn't piece together.

"So, what's it going to be," Col. Status had said to Pinkus, after his eyes finished searching for the now vaporized permit. "Are you going to come along with me peacefully. Or will I have to drag you?"

"But Michael Molecule's concert is going to start at any moment. I can't go anywhere."

"Resisting arrest," Status replied, "that's all I needed to know."

With that Status had hammered Pinkus on his wide neutrolite head with a laser stick, and Pinkus had fallen to the floor, only to wake up at Galactic Police Headquarters, explaining why he hadn't purchased a permit to keep out of jail. And now, with Col. Status at his doorstep again, Pinkus wasn't about to be tricked into another needless trip and interrogation down at Galactic Headquarter, so he politely invited Col. Status in, but walked straight over to the telephone.

"Who are you calling?" asked Status in a gruff voice.

"Click Dark," Pinkus replied. "I'm sure you'd like to explain to him why I won't be able to set up the equipment on Mercury's Strata Lounge tonight. Or haven't you heard," said Pinkus, "I'm the McBison Brothers roadie now. I was hired by Click Dark, himself, only a few minutes ago."

Col. Status rubbed his chin, and Pinkus saw his eyes narrow as he decided what to do. "Don't mess with Dark," was the unofficial rule down at Headquarters, or there will be Cletus to pay.

"Were you just on your way out?" said Pinkus, the telephone receiver in his hand.

"For now," Status replied, putting his sunglasses on the bridge of his nose. "But mark my words, this thing's not over yet."

* * * * * * * * * *

While Michael and Emma landed on the space pad back at Molecule Enterprises, Teaspoon Typhoon gliding Michael's Cosmo IV to a perfect halt, Click Dark, the richest and most influential music promo man in the universe, was instructing his robotan pilot Lilly, a striking neutrolite woman dressed in black leather, to chart a course for Alpha Apus, where he wanted to now personally talk to Dr. Styra Algol about his experiments.

As Lilly made for Click's rendezvous with Dr. Algol, Dr. Algol was standing in his house.

"That's strange," Algol had said to himself, after relating to the Slammy Awards Association the news of his conclusive discovery concerning the effects of the O-Zone Chute music, "they hung up."

Dr. Algol often talked to himself. Henry Otter had heard Dr. Algol's voice earlier, and from Henry's vantage point outside, he hoped that Dr. Algol was indeed talking to himself for he had heard Dr. Algol just tell someone that he had single-handedly discovered the problem of O-Zone Chute music. Henry had done many of the experiments and calculations; hence, he felt that he should be a co-winner of the Slammy Award for Music. But then, Henry had heard Dr. Algol's misgivings at the telephone's bad connection, and now entered to stop Dr. Algol from repeating the same call to the Slammy Awards.

"What's this I heard about you being the sole applicant for the Slammy Award for Music?"

"What about it?" Algol replied, indignantly. "It's my award; I won it."

"Not alone," Henry added, walking slowly over to where Algol stood by the telephone. "I did most of the important calculations and was the guinea pig for the project. All you ever did was make notes on that little clipboard of yours and attached the electrodes to my body. I figure I own one-half of the award."

"Well, you figure wrong, son," Algol stated. "Maybe when you get a little older, and get a lab experiment of your own, you'll realize: the place of experiment determines who owns the discovery. And seeing how that lab on the other side of my house's screen door belongs to me; I believe we can assume that the Slammy Award is rightfully mine."

"But Dr. Algol," Henry said, "it isn't."

"Tell it to someone else," Algol replied, "maybe they'll believe you. But you're wasting your time telling it to me. I've got to call the Slammy Award Association again, then I've got to get out to Mercury's Strata Lounge and prevent what could turn out to be the music universe's biggest disaster."

"What are you talking about?"

"I'm talking about the McBison Brother's O-Zone Chute concert out on Mercury's Strata Lounge tonight. Their expecting to play to a few million humans, and Cletus knows how many robotans will hear it. With that kind of volume, they'll kill all of them."

* * * * * * * * * *

Henry Sloan had taken the telephone call at the Slammy Award Association Office and had hung up on Dr. Algol and had called Click as soon as he had heard the news. It hadn't been hard, Harry Sloan had concluded, for Click Dark to get him situated at Slammy Award Headquarters. Under Click's guidance, Michael Molecule had earned the Slammy Award an unprecedented eleven times with his lyrics found on his now classic Phroton Albums. And Sloan, under Click's direction, didn't have to wait long to receive Dr. Algol's call confirming Click

Dark's worst fear that O-Zone Chute music was indeed bad for everyone's health. As Sloan hung up the telephone, after advising Click of Dr. Algol's findings, he thought about Click's sixth sense for uncanny timing. "Timing in business promotion is everything," Click had once told him. "It can make or break even the smallest of deals." And if Sloan was right, timing was especially important for Click in this case, for with the demise of rock and roll, and Michael Molecule's career, Click Dark had everything on the line. If anything even remotely went sour in regards to the McBisons' concert, Click's business future might very well be ruined. Frankly, Henry Sloan wanted to wash his hands of the whole matter. But until the O-Zone Chute was found to be lethal at high volume concerts, he'd have to play along with Click's game, figuring that riding the fence again between good and evil was at this time in his best interest.

* * * * * * * * * *

It was Michael Molecule's concern about Pinkus, the universe's premiere roadie, that prompted his telephone call to him. Michael and Emma hadn't even been back at Molecule Enterprise Headquarters one minute when Michael was standing next to both Emma and Teaspoon dialing Pinkus' number.

"Hello."

"Pinkus?"

"Yes."

"This is Michael Molecule. How are you?"

"Couldn't be better."

"How's that?" Michael asked. "Usually the recently unemployed aren't so chipper."

"But I'm not."

"Chipper?"

"Unemployed," explained Pinkus. "I picked up a job a few minutes ago with Click Dark doing the sound for the McBison Brothers concert tonight."

"So soon," Michael replied. "I thought Click would at least wait a few days until the Last Chord Concert of rock and roll had at least reached the end of the universe."

"You mean, give it a proper burial?"

"Something like that," Michael said. "So, when are you leaving?"

"Any moment now. The McBisons are using special Three Leap Speakers; ones that will carry the O-Zone Chute over the entire universe."

"That's a little overdoing it, don't you think?"

"You're asking me?" said Pinkus.

"That's right. You're the most knowledgeable sound robotan in the business, aren't you? Kind of the Universe's Premiere Roadie."

"If you must know," Pinkus replied, still thinking about Molecule's comment, "the special McBison sound system is not only over-kill," replied Pinkus. "It could be dangerous."

"What do you mean?"

"With all this talk about Dr. Algol's frequency tests on the hazards of O-Zone Chute music played at high volume, I'd say that Click Dark, by ordering the music at that volume, just might be endangering the lives of the fans."

"But Algol's tests are not conclusive," Michael said. "I just read that in <u>Universe Today Magazine</u>."

"Maybe not," Pinkus replied, "but they're conclusive enough for me. I don't have to be hit on the head twice to get the message."

"What are you talking about?"

"Nothing that would interest you," Pinkus responded. "Are you going to the McBisons' concert?"

"I don't know. I wasn't, at least not until you mentioned the potential hazards to the fans if they hear high volume O-Zone Chute music."

"Good," Pinkus replied. "I don't have time to talk. I got to get my roadies out to the concert site; it's almost three o'clock."

"I understand," Michael replied, then he hung up.

"That's curious," Michael said, turning to Emma and Teaspoon. "Pinkus and the roadies have gone to work for Click Dark and the McBison Brothers."

"Are they crazy?" Emma replied. "I read somewhere that their O-Zone Chute music might be dangerous."

"Me too," added Teaspoon. "But if Pinkus controls the concert, you can bet that things won't get out of hand. He's a good sound roadie."

"Perhaps the best," Michael said.

"That's right," continued Teaspoon, "and if anyone can spot the hazards of high-volume sound, it's Pinkus."

"Even so," said Emma. "Maybe we better go out there just in case. What do you think, Michael?"

"I think maybe we'll all attend, just to keep an eye on things."

"You won't get an argument from me," Teaspoon replied. "I just hope that Click and the McBisons have the health of their fans in mind."

"That's what I'm worried about too," Michael said. "Warm up the space pod."

* * * * * * * * *

Before Lilly, Click Dark's robotan pilot, was hired by Dark Enterprises, she was working and going to Gemini University, studying the vees that outline the Taurus Bull, hoping to eventually get a job as a map reader for The Commercial Space Pod Organization. But it was Click Dark who had eventually hired her, liking her neutrolite looks and her gender. Click knew that in the pecking order of the universe's social strata, that it was bad enough being a robotan, but it was twice as bad being both a robotan and a woman. Click, however, had not hired Lilly to help the progress of the robotan and woman's equal rights, but to use them against her, something she did not learn of until it was too late to change jobs. At first, Click had treated her royally. He had paid her way through Gemini University, so she could stop working nights as a waitress, and had offered her a future job as both his personal interstellar map reader and pilot. But gradually, Lilly, built in the humanoid sequence, found out Click's true intentions, that she was to fly, say little, and obey, which she had done faithfully for over three years. But lately, after hearing Michael Molecule's Last Chord Concert while piloting her boss to Orion to try and stop it, she felt a greater need for self-expression. She, like all intelligent robotans, knew what Molecule's playing of the last rock and roll chord meant to the future of robotan progress towards equality, and lately she had been a bit more reluctant to carry out Click Dark's orders, especially if they hurt others. Yet, it wasn't an open defiance; she wasn't that stupid, but one of quiet resistance, so far usually showing itself in her slower responses to her boss' commands.

Lilly, under the duress of her thoughts, landed Click Dark's space pod with a bounce on Alpha Apus, the home of Dr. Algol. While Click unbuckled his seatbelt and watched the landing pod steps unfurrow from his Cosmos IV, he also knew of Dr. Algol's findings, thanks to Sloan, who he had dropped at the Slammy Awards Headquarters to stand vigil to await Professor Algol's call. The results of Dr. Algol's experiments had not surprised Click, and it was in a stern manner that his footsteps plodded down the exit stairs of his Cosmos IV, where he placed his feet on the ground adjacent to Dr. Algol's lab. Lilly had remained in the cockpit of Dark's space pod, pretending to click switches after landing, to avoid going with Click. Not much of a protest, she had to admit, but one which helped her to get through one more day of being Click Dark's pilot.

"Dr. Algol?" Click asked, after walking up the tubeway, and seeing a person in a white smock.

"No," replied Henry Otter, just leaving Algol's house. "Dr. Algol's inside. But he's quite busy. We're leaving for the McBison Brothers O-Zone Chute Concert on Mercury."

"I see," Click replied.

"Say," said Henry. "Aren't you Click Dark?"

"Yes, I am," said Click, turning on the charm.

"I've watched your Photo-vision show for years," said Henry. "It's hard to believe that you haven't heard."

"Heard what?" asked Click, playing dumb.

"That the McBison's O-Zone Chute music, if played at high volume, can kill."

"That's enough, Henry," Professor Algol said, suddenly appearing in the tubeway. "Why don't you go clean up the lab?"

"But Dr. Algol . . ."

"It's all right, Henry. I'll take care of this. I'm sure, by now, the whole universe knows of Click Dark's less than honorable intentions. I'm sorry, Mr. Dark," continued the Professor, "but your too late. I already notified the Slammy Awards Headquarters of my findings."

"Is that so," Clark laughed. "And I suppose you got a bad connection, too, when you called?"

"As a matter of fact, I did."

"You idiot," cried Dark. "That wasn't the Slammy Awards personnel; that was my man Sloan intercepting the call. I'm afraid," continued Dark, pulling out a laser pistol, "that your proclamation about the O-Zone Chute has fallen on deaf ears."

"Are you mad?" the Professor shouted.

"Only when it comes to money and my survival in the business world. Now, call your stupid assistant back here. I don't have much time."

* * * * * * * * * *

When Pinkus' old Cluster I space pod arrived outside Mercury's Strata Lounge, he got out, planted his feet on Mercury's soil, and shook his head. The terrain had changed considerably since he last visited the outdoor concert lounge. The high rock and shale had been removed, offering little or no promise of embedding speakers, and Mercury's orbit wasn't right to reach the 15 starlites of volume Click Dark had ordered. Mercury, Pinkus had concluded, was actually faced in the opposite orbit, away from the other planets and directly into deep space, where nowhere near the number of fans lived that would have otherwise been reached, had Mercury's orbit been in the opposite direction. So two problems faced Pinkus: first, he had to erect thirty story platforms, from which he could suspend the special Three Leap Speakers; then he had to erect an 80 story neutrolite shield on Mercury's nearest moon to divert the sound back into interplanetary space, the heavily occupied territory in the galaxy. But for now, he couldn't do much but build the volume control shed, where the six-foot volume knob would be stored and used during the concert.

CHAPTER FIVE

Col. Status hadn't always been a bigot, but his father had been one, and the secret to his ambitions concerning his dislike of Pinkus was rooted deep in his childhood. Always a big kid, Jim Status, the boy who later turned Police Colonel, had to defend himself every day against the threats of larger boys. It became a daily routine for Status to walk home from Explorer High School on Pallallax's west end, expecting a fight, a challenge to his toughness. And over the years, his toughness becoming so ingrained that it eventually overtook every reasonable purpose of his personality. His father, a space pod laborer from Fomalhaut, had taught his son well to guard against the intrusions of others.

"Don't give 'em a starlight's inch," Jimmy Status' father had warned, sticking the galactic boxing gloves on his fists at an early age. "And don't you," he continued, "let nobody tell you no different. The universe is made up of two kinds of people: those that shove and those that shove back harder."

Col. Status was thinking about his father's advice when he left Pinkus' house after his failed attempt to roust Pinkus down to the Space Police Headquarters. To Status' surprise Pinkus was neither unemployed, nor at a lack for powerful friends, as he quickly related to Status by grabbing the telephone to call Click Dark. But Col. Status knew that gaining access to Pinkus to make him humble wouldn't be difficult, not with the McBison Brothers concert on Mercury in just a few hours. So while the information about working for Click Dark and being the McBison Brothers new roadie had temporarily saved Pinkus from Status' wrath at Pinkus' apartment, Status knew that in the long-run that information might indeed be the long-term downfall in his quest to make Pinkus, the robotan, bow to his human demands.

* * * * * * * * *

Harry Sloan, Click Dark's right-hand man, was accustomed to being in the action. Since Click had dropped him off a few hours ago at the Slammy Awards Headquarters, he had dutifully intercepted and transferred the telephone call by Dr. Algol to Click's space pod. Click had had the call intercepted and transferred by Sloan to get a jump on preparing for the O-Zone Chute concert at the Strata Lounge on Mercury, despite the experiments by Dr. Algol and his assistant Henry. But Click had had other plans, and as he held Dr. Algol and his assistant Henry Otter, at laser gun point, Click now considered himself a desperate man. Michael Molecule, by his playing of the last chord concert, had ended rock and roll, and now his financial salvation, the McBison Brother's O-Zone Chute music, would be no good to him if word spread that it was lethal. For now, at least, Click Dark was sure that he could control the spread of the effects of O-Zone Chute music to Dr. Algol and his assistant, but as he stood there, his laser gun pointed point black at Dr. Algol and Henry, he wasn't sure that he could kill them.

"So, get it over with," Dr. Algol said, looking Click straight in the eye.

"Get what over with?" Henry, Algol's assistant asked.

"Come on, Henry, said Algol, "this is no time to be naïve. Dark plans to kill us both because we know too much about the effects of his precious O-Zone Chute music."

"That's right," Click replied. "But I'm not going to do it here. That would create too many questions for the Interstellar Police. I'm going to let you become the first victims of O-Zone Chute "Volume Thrust," the music disease that will eventually kill millions at the McBison's concert."

"If you were smart," said Algol, "you'd control the McBisons and have them play only at half volume. You could say that you were creating demand."

"That was my original intention," Click replied. "But after visiting the McBisons at their villa on Corona Borealis, it's pretty obvious to me that they can't be trusted, especially Don, that hothead and Space Blaster hound would never listen to reason."

"You're probably right," Dr. Algol said. "But can't you see that the gig is up. Too many people know about the effects of the O-Zone Chute. You'll never get away with it. What about your man who intercepted the call at Slammy Headquarters? He knows, and he'll tell others."

"Let me be the judge of that," Click said. "Now get into my space pod. We're going to the concert."

Click had concealed his laser gun from Lilly's view during his conversation with Dr. Algol and Henry outside of the space pod by holding the laser gun directly in front of him and close to his body, his back to the spacecraft. So, when Click entered with Dr. Algol and Henry walking in front of him, Lilly had no idea that Dr. Algol and Henry were being taken hostage. The thought never actually occurred to her, until Click had slammed the Cosmos IV door shut, and then turned to hold the laser gun on her as well.

"Take us to Mercury's Strata Lounge and the McBison Brothers' concert and make it at warp nine. Lilly knew better than to argue with her human boss, so she just trained her eyes out through the space pod's front windshield, threw a few switches, and in a moment they were headed towards Mercury faster than any space pod in the universe.

* * * * * * * * *

Michael Molecule' space pod, also a Cosmos IV, was a newer model than Click's, and at the helm Michael had Teaspoon Tyshoon, the best intergalactic pilot in the universe. Teaspoon was used to taking short cuts, like the one he was now taking towards Mercury, with both Michael and Emma aboard. Teaspoon had learned that often shortcuts through the galaxy at warp plus nine speed could mean life or death, and as he cruised Michael's Cosmos IV up to warp nine interplanetary speed, he had a funny feeling that this might indeed be a case of life and death. As Teaspoon manipulated the controls, revving the fifty photon energy cells for every light of power they possessed, Michael and Emma sat comfortably in the back of the space pod watching the universe go by outside their window. They were sitting close together again, holding hands, and Michael, closest to the window stared blankly out into space with a strange, almost terrified look on his face.

"Don't worry, Michael," Emma said, "we'll stop Click and the McBisons before they perform."

"We better," Michael replied. "Nothing less than the survival of music in the universe depends on it."

"What do you mean?"

"If Click succeeds in getting the McBisons on stage to play, he'll be the wealthiest man in the universe at the expense of ending all music. If the O-Zone Chute music doesn't kill all the people, the volume will certainly make them deaf."

"That's scary," Emma replied.

"It's hard to believe that Click would continue the concert knowing the repercussions of his actions."

"That's it," said Emma.

"That's what?" Michael asked.

"Repercussions. It's the answer to our problem. Have you been to Mercury's Strata Lounge lately?"

"Not since I opened for the McBison Brothers years ago, when I first got out of the army. Why?"

"The place has changed," Emma said. "The rock face that once provided an ideal spot for speaker implant is now gone. But beyond that, Mercury's orbit is not right. When Click had to move up the McBison Brothers concert, he had everything figured out. But he missed one small detail: the McBison Brothers O-Zone Chute music and the light beam that carries it will be aimed out into deep space, and not at an interplanetary audience. For it to have any interplanetary direction at all, it will have to be reflected by at least an eighty story neutrolite screen place on Mercury's second moon."

"She's right," said Teaspoon, looking back from the cockpit. "This time of the interstellar year, Mercury is definitely faced in the wrong direction for good interplanetary sound."

"So, all we have to do is to contact Pinkus, and have him discontinue the construction of the neutrolite shield. I heard he's taken a job there."

"Or make it too short," added Teaspoon, "so that the sound passes over it, and is not rebounded by it."

* * * * * * * * * *

Pinkus, the universe's chief roadie, was an efficient robotan. Not long after he arrived at the concert site, his 3,000 robotan roadies were busily readying the site for the McBison Brothers concert. Pinkus managed the building of the stage, and the construction of the volume knob shed himself, and oversaw the construction of the neutrolite deflector screen on Mercury's second moon by using telepathic communications. And as the construction continued, Click Dark, holding Lilly and Dr. Algol hostage, pointed to an interstellar map, indicating Lilly to make for Romus to pick up Sloan at the Slammy Awards Headquarters.

"There won't be enough time to pick up Sloan and make it to the concert," Lilly replied, after seeing Click's index finger pointing towards the map.

"You better make time, then," Click replied, "because your life as well as theirs depends on it."

"Don't do it," Henry yelled to Lilly. "He has to kill us all anyway because of our precious knowledge."

"Knowledge," said Lilly.

"That O-Zone Chute music at high volume is lethal."

"Nice going, Henry," Dr. Algol replied. "You just condemned that nice robotan pilot to die with us."

"I think you both better quit talking," Click said and with that he gagged them with their own handkerchiefs and tied them to their chairs by winding an electrical cord around them. "Now, fly this crate," Click yelled at Lilly. "We have to be the first to arrive at the concert site."

* * * * * * * * * *

While Harry Sloan waited to be picked up at the Slammy Awards Headquarters on Romus, a phone call from Click confirmed his reservation on Click's Cosmos IV, along with Lilly, Dr. Algol and Henry. Harry sat in the Glass Dome Lounge, near the launch pad, a Space Blaster in his hand. What a day, he thought, wrapped up in his own thoughts, as sure as the cords around the chests of Dr. Algol and Henry. First, the deal with Big Star Enterprises had soured, his relationship with Click Dark threatened because of his conversation with Emma at the Leo Minor Lounge, and now here he waited for Click to pick him up to go to the McBison Brothers concert, despite the knowledge of the music being lethal. Frankly, he thought, he didn't want to be anywhere near Mercury's Strata Lounge when the McBison Brothers cut loose with their O-Zone Chutes, but like always, he figured that Click had brought him this far and he would hang with him a little while longer despite the circumstances.

Harry Sloan was working on his second Space Blaster when from a distance out the huge glass dome, he saw the unmistakable green flashing light on the nose of Click Dark's Cosmos IV. Green lights, as everyone knew in the universe, were only attached to the Cosmos IV, and only to their most expensive models, those ranging in price from two to four million zercons. Harry watched Click's space pod grow from a tiny blinking green dot in interstellar space into a full-sized Cosmos IV landing on the launch pad outside the lounge window, gulped his second Space Blaster, and rushed to greet it.

"Get in," Click yelled to Harry, waving his laser pistol as soon as the Cosmos IV's boarding steps had unfolded.

Confused, Harry entered the Cosmos IV, his hands raised.

"Now, sit down Harry and enjoy your last ride through the galaxy."

"But why, Click? I'm your friend," asked Harry, sitting down and looking across the aisle at Dr. Algol and Henry bound and gagged.

"Because you know too much."

"But Click, you know me. I won't talk."

"That's right, Harry," Click said, motioning with his gun for Lilly to take off. "I do know you, and it's exactly because I do that you're here, and will be one of the first to go. Now, just sit there and shut up, or I'll have to bind and gag you, too, just like your fellow passengers."

Harry Sloan sat back in his chair. Tears came into his eyes. He hadn't bargained on this. He wasn't a big fish, someone so important or successful that it would warrant this action against him. He wanted to tell Click this, too, but he knew how Click Dark's mind worked: he should have known not to meet him, but his business mind and greed had once again overridden his good judgement.

* * * * * * * * *

While Click Dark's space pod Cosmos IV sped towards to Mercury's Strata Lounge and the concert site, Michael and Emma's space pod was nearing the concert site, with everything seemingly under control.

"Good," yelled Teaspoon from the cockpit. "Click Dark's space pod has not landed yet."

"And when it does," Michael replied, "you can expect all Cletus to break loose."

"What do you mean?"

"I mean if Click doesn't see our space pod, he'll surely see that Pinkus' neutrolite shield from Mercury's second moon is not tall enough. He might be desperate, but he's not stupid."

"You're right," Emma said. "Isn't there some way to conceal the pod, and the height of the shield?"

"Only if you're a magician," Michael replied. "From the space approach to Mercury any pilot could see either another space craft or the neutrolite shield size without much trouble."

"There's got to be a way," said Emma. "Let's ask Pinkus."

If Michael, Emma, and Teaspoon had known the hostage circumstance on board Click Dark's spacecraft, they would have counted on Lilly's eyes to ease Dark's space pod into the Mercury landing lane, nose first, thus avoiding Click's detection of the presence of either their spacecraft or the low neutrolite shield. Click, with so many prisoners aboard, was having his hands full just watching Sloan.

"What's the matter, Sloan. Afraid to die?"

"Afraid of dying friendless," blubbered Sloan, his face hidden in his hands.

"Now, now," crooned Click in a mocking manner, "won't the great Cletus accept you into his arms if your friendless?"

"He might, but it probably would have been a little easier, if I had been a little more Cletus-like."

"Stardust!" yelled Click, "that's what all that Cletus hocus-pocus is . . . just stardust!"

* * * * * * * * * *

By now, Pinkus had the concert site completely readied for the arrival of the McBisons. His robotan roadies had split the two-atom atmosphere with electron jackhammers and had shimmed in two eighty story Three leap Speakers into Mercury's bedrock. Dwarfed by the speakers, Pinkus smiled at the completion of moving the speakers into place and then radioed out to his roadies on Mercury's second moon to check on the setting up of the neutrolite shield.

"How's it going?" Pinkus yelled into his telepathic walkaround.

"We're having a bit of a problem," a tiny voice replied, obviously from one of the four-foot tall, green robotans manufactured later, after the neutrolite mined at Pegasus falls had started to dwindle.

"What kind of a problem?" Pinkus asked.

"The atmosphere is almost too dense to hold up a neutrolite reflector. Mercury's second moon is faced in the wrong direction; it's orbit angle is off."

"I know," responded Pinkus, sympathizing with his roadie. "But we must get that neutrolite shield erected, and we're running out of time."

Pinkus looked at his planetary watch; it was 7:45 p.m. Fifteen minutes to concert time, and still no complete eighty story shield, or sign of Click Dark and his space pod.

"Great Cletus," yelled Pinkus through his telepathic walkaround, after checking the time. "Do I have to come out there and personally erect that shield?"

"No sir," squeaked the voice at the other end. "We'll get it up, one way or another."

* * * * * * * * * *

At exactly 7:55 p.m., Teaspoon landed Michael's space pod on the landing pad next to the Strato Lounge on Mercury. And without delay, the exit steps dropped from it, and Michael, Emma, and Teaspoon ran towards Pinkus, who was just putting the finishing touches on the control shield.

"Here for the concert?" Pinkus asked, a studious look aimed at the volume control knob in the shed.

"No," cried Michael, "we're here to stop it."

"Why on Cletus' name would you want to do that?"

"Because the McBisons' O-Zone Chute music can kill."

"Is that fact?"

"Almost, we fear that Dr. Algol, the scientist on Alpha Apus, has found conclusive evidence, and that tonight's concert could be lethal."

"I got 3,000 of the universe's best robotan roadies not 100,000 miles from here over on Mercury's second moon erecting a neutrolite shield."

"That's why we're here," said Emma. "We want to take down the shield."

"That's impossible, I'm afraid," Pinkus replied. "I just told my crew to speed up its erection. It's probably finished by now. Let me check."

* * * * * * * * * *

While Pinkus was telepathically checking on the neutrolite shield's completion on Mercury's second moon, Click Dark's spacecraft cruised in at wave-length speed, just over the tops of Mercury's Actus Mountains, and abruptly stopped, not far from where Michael, Emma, and Teaspoon were speaking with Pinkus. Pinkus was the first to turn and see Click marching everyone he had taken hostage, including the McBisons, forward with a gun at their backs.

"Trouble," Pinkus said, motioning his hand for Michael to look at Click, who was approaching, laser pistol in hand.

Michael, Emma, and Teaspoon turned just as Click Dark approached, his two front hostages, Dr. Algol and his assistant Henry, still bound and gagged, leading the way for a shaken Harry Sloan and a quiet Lilly and McBison brothers.

"Don't tell me," Michael said, as Click and his hostages came to a halt, "the O-Zone Chute music really is lethal."

"That's right," Click replied, now holding his laser pistol on them. "And besides us, there is no one else in the universe who knows about it. And no one's going to know, either, at least not until I get my due for setting up the universe's last musical concert."

"That's what this is really about. Isn't it?" Michael said. "You don't give a Cletus about the money. You just want to end all music and secure a spot in music's immortality."

"That's right, kid. And at one time I thought you wanted the same thing. But I guess I was wrong."

"I guess you were," Michael replied, looking at Emma.

"Enough talk," cried Click. "Pinkus, what's the status on the sound equipment?"

"It's definitely not ready yet," Pinkus replied. "They're having some problems over on Mercury's second moon erecting the neutrolite sound shield."

"You better go over there and help them," replied Click.

"And if I don't?"

"Then you'll never see your friends alive again."

"Don't do it," Michael yelled. "He's going to kill us all anyway."

"That's right," said Teaspoon, who had eased into a spot next to Lilly.

Pinkus looked at the frightened faces of his friends, people who had kept him and his robotan friends working as roadies for eons, and he just didn't have the heart to be the direct cause for their death, so he left, lifting his old Cluster I space pod off the launch pad.

"You'll never get away with this," Michael said, after Pinkus had left.

"Sure I will," Click replied. "Just watch me." Then, he motioned for all of them to squeeze into the control shed, which housed the six-foot diameter volume knob.

* * * * * * * * * *

On his way over to Mercury's second moon, Pinkus thought he had seen another space pod heading in the same direction. Yet, he didn't know whose it was until he landed.

"Col. Status," Pinkus said, after exiting his space pod, parked over a small rise from the shield site, "what are you doing here?"

"That's a strange question coming from you," replied Col. Status, meeting Pinkus at the bottom of his pace pod stairway and drawing his laser pistol. "I told you our little battle wasn't over. You might have won the last round at your apartment by threatening to call Click Dark on the phone, but up here, I'm the one with the laser pistol."

"Listen, Status, there's too much at stake right now. Click Dark is planning to murder millions of innocent humans and robotans with the McBison Brothers' O-Zone Chute music."

"You expect me to believe that," Status replied.

"It's true. I swear it," Pinkus replied, a hint of terror in his voice.

"That's more like it," replied Status, listening to Pinkus' voice becoming unglued at the hinges.

"What's with you and your obsession of who's equal in the universe?"

"It's an unwritten law," Status replied, "that some creatures are placed higher on the scale than others."

"And you and your bigotry rest somewhere near the bottom rung of the ladder," said Pinkus. "You've got to believe me. If I don't get this neutrolite shield erected in the next two minutes, five innocent people, including Michael Molecule, are going to die."

"So, what's five people," laughed Status, "if what you say about the McBisons' music is true?"

"Five or one," Pinkus replied. "Don't you see? The taking of any life, robotan or human is immoral."

"You say, Michael Molecule is being held by Click Dark?"

"That's right. Please, you've got to help me!"

"Get down on one knee and say pretty please," Status replied. "Then I might."

Knowing what was at stake, and that his battle with Status wasn't something solved in one day, Pinkus quickly kneeled and gave Status his response. Then Status followed Pinkus over the shale rise on Mercury's second moon to finish erecting the neutrolite shield.

* * * * * * * * * *

"Now," said Click Dark, sarcastically, "are you all nice and cozy?"

Michael, tied to the huge volume knob along with the other hostages, looked at Click's maniacal face in the doorway of the control shed. Click had the McBison Brothers at gun point and was leading them a short distance away to the stage, which had been emptied by Pinkus on Click's orders before he left. There were no screaming fans, not a sound, as Click, with Michael and the others safely tied to the volume knob, went up the elevator to center stage.

"We just won't do what he says," cried Lilly, tied securely next to Teaspoon.

"I'm afraid we'll have to," Michael replied. "At least for a little while until I can figure out what to do."

"If we start walking in a circle tied to this volume knob like Click wants us to do, we'll gradually increase the O-Zone Chute music and cause our own demise."

"That's what he's got planned," said Michael.

"I say we simply don't do it," Lilly said. "After all, he's going to kill us anyway."

"But if we don't," Teaspoon replied, "Click will just come back in here immediately and kill us anyway. This way, at least Michael gets a chance to think."

* * * * * * * * *

As Pinkus led Col. Status over the rock surface of Mercury's second moon towards the neutrolite shield, they could both see that Pinkus' help would not be needed to secure the erection of the neutrolite shield. It had already been done for them by the regular universe roadies.

"I thought you said there was a problem up here?" Status said.

"There was," Pinkus replied. "But now, the problem is not up here, it's down there, back at the Strata Lounge on Mercury's surface, where Michael and the others are being held hostage."

"Come on," said Status. "I'm not going to follow you all over the Mercury surface looking for phantoms."

"Even if it could mean a promotion?"

"Promotion?" asked the Colonel.

"Off hand, I'd say, anyone who saved the universe from a mass murderer would be eligible for a promotion."

Status twisted his moustache. Finally, he dropped his hand. "Maybe you're right," he said. "Let's get on down to Mercury in my Space Cruiser and have a look. But don't try no funny stuff. I'm the one with the laser pistol."

* * * * * * * * *

"How much longer?" shouted Click at the McBison Brothers. "For Cletus sake, we've been on stage long enough for you to rev up the light beam sound jacks. What's the problem?"

"The problem" replied Don McBison, pie-eyed from sniffing an afternoon's worth of Space Blasters, "is that I don't like the idea of being blasted into sound smithereens by my own music. How are you going to escape?"

"It's too late for talk," Click replied. "Just do as you're told, or I'll zap you right now."

Phil, the older of the McBison Brothers, hooked up the last laser sound jack, and both McBisons nodded to Click, who waved his laser pistol in their faces. Then Click spoke into the telepathic walkaround he had taken from Pinkus.

"Okay," came his voice over the sound wave speaker in the control shed, "you can start walking now. And I better see a rapid increase in the volume, or I'll be up there to do things more abruptly."

Michael and the others, all tied to the six-foot control knob, started walking in a circle.

"I want you to know," Teaspoon said walking behind Michael, "that if we don't get out of this, that I've always considered you my best friend."

"Thanks," Michael responded, "but I've got an idea. Let's reverse our direction and walk the other way."

"What?" asked Emma.

"I get it," Teaspoon replied, stopping. "If we reverse the flow of the volume, it will actually reduce their power."

"Why didn't Click think of that when he tied us up here?" Lilly asked.

"Because for years he's been letting other people earn his money for him. He knows nothing about the mechanics of a concert site, except perhaps that a neutrolite shield would be necessary. But any first-year roadie would know that."

Suddenly, everyone in the group stopped and began circling in the opposite direction, just as Pinkus and Col. Status arrived at the shed door.

"What are you doing?" Pinkus asked, seeing the group willingly pushing the six-foot volume knob faster. Then Pinkus noticed their direction.

"Good thinking," Pinkus said. "It's pure genius."

"What are they doing?" Status asked, wondering how people tied up against their will could be so happy.

"They're turning back the musical clock," said Pinkus. "Attached to this volume knob is the progression of music since its beginning. The light waves it controls, not only can focus sound forward in time, as in the concert tonight, but one so large also has the power to regather sound as well."

"Make it go backwards?" asked Status.

"That's right," said Pinkus. "And without the forward movement of sound, Click and the McBison Brothers' O-Zone Chute music is out of business. Now, the only question is: how far back in music history do these people want to take the universe?"

"How about all the way back to the beginnings of rock and roll," said Michael.

"Do you mean it!" shouted Emma, "You could start your career all over again. This time with me at your side."

"And us, too," Teaspoon replied, looking at Lilly.

"Don't forget us," replied Dr. Algol and Henry, after Col. Status had ripped off their gags, "for the universe needs a safe sound."

Then Michael looked at Harry Sloan. "You'll have to change," Michael said. "Every deal is above board."

"Above board, honest!" Harry said.

"Well then," Michael replied, "it looks like we're back in the business of rock and roll. Then Col. Status left them, and headed for the stage to get Click Dark, while Pinkus thought about how nice it would be to have work for a lifetime.

THE END

9 789389 690781